DARK SPIRITS: THE WATCHER

LEE MOUNTFORD

FREE BOOK

Sign up to my mailing list for free horror books...

Want more scary stories? Sign up to my mailing list and receive your free copy of *The Nightmare Collection - Vol 1* as well as *Inside: Perron Manor* (a prequel novella to *Haunted: Perron Manor*) directly to your email address.

The novel-length short story collection and prequel novella are sure to have you sleeping with the lights on.

Sign up now.

www.leemountford.com

1

'SO, ANY QUESTIONS?' JODIE CALLAGHAN ASKED AS SHE LOOKED out at the faces staring back at her. A hand went up. 'Yes?'

'Are we going to be doing seances and things like that?' the young woman with her hand up asked.

Jodie guessed the woman was somewhere in her twenties. She was wrapped up in a duffle coat with a wool hat pulled down over her ears. Everyone present was decked out in similar warm clothing.

'We will,' Jodie confirmed. 'But first, now that you all know how to use the equipment, we'll give you a little time to explore the building on your own. But remember, stick to groups of no less than two. In about an hour or so, we'll regroup and run some seance sessions.'

The young woman smiled and turned to the friend she'd come with. They giggled excitedly.

'Now remember,' Tony Bullock began from his position next to Jodie. 'While rooms six, seven, and eight are supposed to have the most activity, there have been reports *all* over the building, so don't feel the need to rush to the main hotspots. They'll get overcrowded if everyone just makes a beeline straight for those three rooms.'

Tony was Jodie's business partner as well as an old friend. At fifty-five years old, he was seventeen years her senior. She had known him for a long time, and they had set up the ghost hunting venture back when Mark was alive.

Spirit Hunters.

While the name wasn't the most original, it was the only one the three of them had been able to settle on back in the day. The organisation had been in business for just over ten years now, yet had never come close to being able to support them full time.

That wasn't the point of it, of course. It was a passion. A calling.

There had been a hiatus after Mark had died, and at one point Jodie didn't think she'd ever be able to go back to ghost hunting, but eventually she'd pushed herself to try it again and had found it brought her comfort.

The group of eight patrons started to disperse, forming into three clusters: the girl and her friend as one, then two groups of three. They all had various pieces of equipment Jodie and Tony had brought with them: thermal cameras, EVP recorders, and EMF meters. Jodie saw Tony watch with trepidation as the would-be ghost hunters started fiddling with the company's expensive instruments.

'They won't break anything,' Jodie playfully whispered to him.

'I know,' Tony said, his face a frown.

'Then relax.'

Tony had always been overly protective of the equipment, which was understandable. It was expensive to replace, and plenty of it had been damaged over the years, but Jodie knew that was just the cost of business. If people had to bring all their own gear—which they sometimes did anyway—then *Spirit Hunters* wouldn't get half as many customers. Being given the toys to play with was all part of the experience.

Once everyone had left the main bar area of the Manor House pub, Tony approached the bar, where he'd placed his thermos; he poured Jodie and himself a steaming cup of black coffee before adding sugar to Jodie's. Jodie cupped her hands around the polystyrene cup and took a sip, the warmth welcome against the cold.

'Think we'll see anything tonight?' Tony asked her.

Jodie shrugged. 'Maybe. We've picked up a few voices here before, so we might get the same again.'

This was the twelfth time *Spirit Hunters* had run an event at the pub. They knew the owners, so it was easy to get sessions booked—all they had to do was give the owners a small fee.

The Manor House was well known in its local village of Ferryhill, with prior owners and even patrons telling stories of paranormal activity. The son of one prior owner had supposedly been thrown from his bed by an unseen force. Disembodied voices were common, and one man told of how, when at the urinal, he'd heard the main door open and close, followed by footsteps heading into a cubicle. He'd also claimed to have felt the air move as an unseen person walked past. However, when the man had checked the open cubicle, no one was there.

While it was an interesting location for Jodie, she felt things there had become stale. She and Tony had four venues that they hit regularly on a rotation every few months, but they needed something else. Something new.

And Jodie had a special place in mind. But it would be for her and her alone. She didn't intend to tell Tony of her plan—he wouldn't like it.

Jodie was going to return to Parson Hall.

'It'll be four years for Mark tomorrow,' Tony said, voice low. Her pulse quickened. Did he know about her plan?

'Yeah,' Jodie said with a slight nod. She kept her eyes on her cup.

'How are things? You doing okay?'

'As well as I can,' was all she said. She knew Tony wanted to hear she was doing fine, because she knew the older man worried about her. It was sweet, but the truth was she would never be fine again. Not really.

Life was different now.

Even though it had been four years, she was still just coping, getting by. She'd found that as time progressed, grief affected her in ways she hadn't anticipated. She still missed her husband terribly, but after the raw anguish immediately following his death, she'd realised she was left with a black hole in her stomach that just couldn't be filled. There was a numbness to her. It wasn't like she didn't feel at all, but the edges of sensations were dulled. Joy wasn't as joyful, laughter wasn't as hearty, and excitement wasn't as invigorating.

'I know I keep saying it,' Tony went on, 'but if you ever need anything—'

'Then I can just ask,' Jodie finished for him with a smile. 'I know, Tony, and I appreciate that. But I just have to keep moving on. Things are different than I'd thought they'd be, and it is what it is. But don't worry, I'm coping.'

'Okay,' he said. 'Just checking in. I won't keep going on about it.'

The bar area they were in was large and mostly dark, save for the electric lights she and Tony had positioned around the space. The area was their headquarters for the night, but later on they would plunge it into complete darkness to perform a seance. Not that they'd experienced much in the bar before specifically, the only real sign of activity there being a spike in an EMF reading a year ago. Their best results had come from the three most notorious rooms, and also the cellar.

Thankfully, given it was summer, the nights weren't too cold, even with the heating in the building off. While they all still needed to wrap up warm, it was far more manageable than the events the pair ran during the winter.

'We need some new locations,' Tony said, as if mirroring Jodie's earlier thoughts. She looked over at him. Standing at five-nine, the man was actually an inch shorter than Jodie. He had a smattering of grey stubble that was too thin and patchy to be designer, and a shaven head that he always hid beneath caps or hats. He was in good shape thanks to a regiment of regular cycling, though Jodie had always thought his cheeks looked a little gaunt.

She nodded in response to his statement. 'Yeah, I was just thinking that,' she said. 'I mean, the places in the usual rotation are great, but we could do with something to spice it up.'

'I was thinking about Parson Hall the other day,' he went on. Jodie's body tensed up, though she hid it well.

'Oh yeah, why?'

'Because of the experience we had there, why else?' he replied. 'Did you know English Heritage is going to be picking it up?'

'Yeah, I'd heard,' she said. 'They'll take ownership in the next few weeks, right?'

'Correct. And when they do, there goes any hope we have of getting back there again. Shame.'

'In fairness, it's been off-limits for a while, ever since it was bought by the Eggertons. They shut down ghost-hunting there pretty quickly.'

'Yeah, and they ran it into the ground,' Tony said. 'It was never going to work as a guest house. Too many people had tried before.'

'Too many guests reported strange things happening,'

Jodie added. 'They'd have been better trying to lean into the haunted aspect, rather than trying to ignore it.'

Tony chuckled. 'I'd have loved to get back one day. The experience we had there will probably never be topped. But I guess I should let it go for good now. It isn't going to happen.' He looked at Jodie. 'You okay with that? I know it was kinda special for you and Mark.'

'I… wouldn't say special,' she lied. 'We had a strong experience there—'

'Which resulted in him popping the question!' Tony interrupted with another laugh.

Jodie smiled. 'True. Strange place to propose—on a ghost hunt.'

'But pretty fitting for Mark.'

'Also true,' Jodie said, still smiling. 'But no, I'm fine with it being sold off. It is what it is. Though since the Eggertons went bankrupt, it's just standing empty, and there will be no power to any security cameras or anything. It might actually be the perfect time to…' She let the words hang.

Tony frowned. 'You're not suggesting breaking in, are you?'

Jodie chuckled and playfully punched his arm. 'I'm kidding, Tony. Of course not.'

Tony's frown melted away, replaced by a grin. 'Ah,' he said. 'Yeah, you got me. I mean, the last thing we need as a company is getting both our directors locked up for trespassing.'

'Of course. Would have been fun to see it at night one last time, though.'

'It would have,' Tony agreed. 'Shame we can't.'

Yeah... shame we can't.

After the patrons had finished their own mini-investigations, they all gathered back into the main bar area.

'Anyone have any interesting experiences?' Tony asked the crowd.

'We picked up some cold spots in the cellar,' one woman said, clearly excited.

'Us too,' another man added.

The young woman that had asked about seances earlier then raised her hand. 'I think me and my friend heard a… voice,' she said. 'But we didn't manage to get a recording.'

'A voice?' Jodie asked. 'Really? That's interesting. Where were you?'

'In room six,' the woman replied.

'What did it say?' Tony asked.

The two women looked at each other before the answer came from the other one. 'It was hard to make out, but we think it was 'bring her' or something like that.'

'Bring her?' Tony echoed. 'Strange. Did the voice sound young or old? Male or female?'

'I… think it was a child's voice,' the girl replied. 'Don't know if it was a boy or girl.'

Jodie watched the two women, specifically how they kept glancing at each other with nervous frowns. Their excitement from earlier had completely disappeared. *They're freaked out.*

'Okay,' Tony went on. 'That's good to know. Sounds like you two had a really great encounter. Not many people get that. Is this your first time ghost hunting?' The girls nodded, looking a little hesitant. Tony's eyes widened. 'Wow, hearing voices on your first time, that's great!'

Jodie could tell her business partner, clueless as always, hadn't picked up on their apprehension.

'It can be scary, can't it?' Jodie asked gently. The girls gave slow nods. 'It's okay,' Jodie continued. 'Just remember, nothing here can hurt you. But there's no shame in being afraid. Hell, it's still my go-to emotion whenever I experience activity. Just try to look past that. You had an amazing experience there, something to look back on. Are you both okay carrying on?'

The pair turned to one another once more for reassurance, then Jodie was met with assertive nods.

'We are,' the first girl said. 'It just... really creeped us out.'

'And that's fine,' Jodie said. 'Don't feel bad about it, but do try to push through.'

'Now,' Tony began, changing the subject as he clapped his gloved hands together, 'how about we run some seance sessions? We can split into two groups. Jodie will lead half of you up to room six, and the other half will come down to the cellar with me. During the sessions, we'll take turns being in the rooms alone.'

'Alone?' the first girl said, eyes widening with worry.

'Or in small groups,' Jodie quickly added. 'You can go in with your friend. It's only for ten minutes, or less if you want to come back out. We'll be right outside. Or you can just skip it if you want, there's no pressure.'

After a brief pause, the girl replied with, 'Okay.'

The patrons split into the two groups, the girl and her friend among those that went with Jodie up to room six.

While the Manor House mainly operated as a pub, it still had rooms to rent out upstairs and also offered bed-and-breakfast services, though according to the owners, guests were few and far between, given Ferryhill was a sleepy little town.

Jodie took her group up and entered room six, which had a basic decor: white wallpaper with embossed patterns, a double bed with a black leather headboard, light brown curtains, a black three-seat sofa that didn't look particularly comfortable, and a tall chest of drawers opposite the foot of the bed. There was a small television standing on top of the drawers, with the remote control just in front of it.

The sessions ran for the next hour, ten to fifteen minutes each time, with the people inside asking questions aloud and trying to communicate. However, the only thing anyone reported was one of the men saying he'd heard a slight shuffling sound coming from inside the room with him.

After that, the two teams regrouped and performed some EVP recordings before giving everyone some more free time. Everything was brought to a close a little after one in the morning.

Once all the patrons had left for the night, seemingly all happy having enjoyed their experience, Jodie and Tony began to pack up.

'Not a whole lot of activity tonight,' Tony said as he placed a camera back into its case.

'Some,' Jodie said, 'but yeah, a fairly quiet night. The voice those girls heard would have been great if it had been recorded.'

'I'm still not convinced those girls actually heard anything,' Tony said. He then looked to her. 'Want to run a few seances ourselves before we go?'

Jodie considered it. Doing a few sessions after the customers had gone was pretty standard, and a perk of the job—she loved showing people the ropes, but there was nothing like running a personal investigation in a haunted location. 'Would Alice be okay with that?' Jodie asked.

Alice was Tony's wife. She was a woman Jodie knew well, and someone she really liked, but Jodie was aware Alice had absolutely zero interest in the paranormal. Even so, Alice still supported her husband in his passion, claiming it was no different from a partner that was obsessed with golf, only it meant a few more late nights.

'Yeah, she'll be fine,' Tony said. 'She'll be asleep in bed by now anyway, so it's no problem.'

'Then sure, sounds good,' Jodie said. 'I've got no plans tomorrow, so I can sleep in.'

'Where do you wanna try? The cellar?'

Jodie cocked her head to the side, thinking. 'Room six, I think,' she replied. 'One of the guys here heard shuffling, and that's where those two girls heard the voice as well.'

'*Supposedly* heard the voice,' Tony replied. 'What was it they said they heard? 'Bring her,' or something, right?'

'That's right.'

'So, what do you think that meant?'

'No idea,' Jodie said.

'Those two looked like they got spooked easily,' Tony went on. 'It could have just been an echo from my group downstairs or something, a voice travelling up, you know?'

'Well, they seemed to be sure,' Jodie said. 'But we'll never know for certain.'

After finally getting everything packed up and loaded into the car, the pair re-entered the pub and moved upstairs. A minute later, they stood in the corridor just outside room six, both with flashlights in hand. A black metal number six was fixed loosely to the surface of the white-panelled door.

'You wanna go first?' Tony asked her.

'Nope,' Jodie replied. 'You go. I'm happy to wait.'

And waiting meant waiting *directly* outside the room. That was one of their unwritten rules during investigations. Always had been, even stretching back to when Mark was involved: nothing was done solo. Seances sometimes needed private spaces, but that didn't mean the other person wasn't as close by as possible.

While investigating the paranormal wasn't usually dangerous, measures still needed to be taken—they were both well aware things could get precarious. The incident back in Parson Hall was testament to that.

And yet, Jodie was planning to abandon that rule soon enough.

Is it the right thing to do? she wondered.

Tony went inside. She heard him move around for a little bit before things got silent. Remaining outside the door, Jodie waited and listened. Soon, Tony started talking, asking the spirit to show itself, asking why it felt throwing a boy out of his bed at night was appropriate.

Despite being a seasoned investigator, Jodie hadn't been lying to the girl earlier when she said she still got spooked. The fear of the unknown was always there, *always*, yet every time she'd found a way to push through.

Because despite being scared, nothing she'd witnessed so far, not even the incident in Parson Hall, came close to what had happened to Jodie as a child at her grandma's house.

The nightmares from that incident still lingered. That was where her interest in the paranormal was first born, and why she treated the matter with such respect.

Then why am I throwing safety to the wind and going back to Parson Hall alone?

She knew why, of course.

Mark.

Maybe it was stupid—it *was* stupid—but this was the last chance she'd have to go back there and explore the place. And she didn't feel the hall was dangerous, really. Active? Yes. But not dangerous. Not like at her grandma's.

And Parson Hall *had* meant a lot to Jodie, despite what she'd said to Tony. It was the place her husband had proposed, late at night, after they'd both been scared half to death. The place where she'd said yes, which had replaced that spike of fear with overwhelming joy.

Stupid as it was, she felt she owed it to her husband, as well as herself, to go back and see the hall again. To see it *alone*. Not with tourists wandering around beside her. It would be a private moment that would hopefully help her let go of some of the pain she'd been carrying around.

After twenty minutes, Tony came out with a glum expression. 'Nothing,' he said. Jodie was half-tempted to forgo her turn and just call it a night. Her eyes had grown heavy, and though she'd become accustomed to returning home quite late following their investigations, at that moment she just wanted to crawl back into her bed and fall asleep until noon.

In the end, though, she pushed herself, like she often did. This time not fighting through fear, but fatigue. After all, she was already there. Why not try one last thing?

So, she went inside and closed the door behind her, using the flashlight to see. She took a seat on the side of the bed and closed her eyes, waiting, forcing herself to keep her breathing even and stay calm. That familiar growing sense of dread had started to creep its way up her spine, so her breathing exercises were a way to combat that. One thing she'd found long ago was that fear also made her feel alive. Scary could be *exciting*, and it was that notion she clung to as she prepared to speak to any spirits that might be present.

She took a breath. 'Is there anybody there?' she said, deliberately loud, hearing Tony chuckle through the door at her use of the clichéd phrase.

'I'm not sure they'd appreciate sarcasm if they *are* there, Jodie,' he said from outside.

Jodie allowed herself to smile and took another breath, forcing more calm over herself. Then, she switched off the torch and waited, just staring into the dark.

After about five minutes of nothing, she felt a cold touch on her hand and gasped.

2

Jodie yanked her hand away, cradling it close to her chest as she sprang up from the bed. She quickly flicked on her torch, casting the beam around the room, her breath caught in her throat.

Though the touch had been brief, it had felt like a small, freezing hand had pressed against her own.

'You okay?' Tony called from the other side of the door.

'F—fine,' Jodie replied. Her eyes darted around the space, but she saw nothing.

Be calm, Jodie told herself. *Slow your breathing.*

'You... don't sound fine,' Tony said loudly. 'Want me to come in?'

'No!' she ordered. 'It's fine, Tony. I... I felt something on my hand. But I'm good, and I wanna see it through. So, just... I need silence again so we don't scare it off, alright?'

'Understood,' came the single-word reply. No more was said.

After waiting for a few more seconds in a standing position, Jodie sat on the bed again. Her heart was racing. She went through her normal mental checks she used to keep herself grounded, then looked for a rational explanation, just to rule out anything obvious.

But she couldn't think of anything.

It certainly hadn't been a draft. She had felt a cold pressure, that of a small hand. Jodie had no doubt about that. A child. She knew it in her gut.

Jodie pulled out her phone, set it to video record, and held it up.

'I'm… here,' Jodie said to the empty space before her, keeping her voice quiet and gentle. 'I'm listening. Is there something you want to tell me?'

She switched off her flashlight and waited. And waited.

Then… she shivered. A cold sensation slowly drifted over her.

Keep calm.

Yet again, her breath caught in her throat—this time as she felt the mattress compress behind her, as if someone had crawled onto it.

Oh my God.

Jodie clenched her teeth together and balled up her fists, her body going completely tense.

'T… Tony,' she said, her voice cracking. 'Something's happening.'

'What? Do you want me to come in?' came the reply.

Yes. 'No,' she called back, trying to keep her voice steady. *This is what you do. Keep control.*

Normally, Jodie would have managed the initial jolt of fear far better, but the regular activity she experienced wasn't on this level. Physical touch and the movement of the bed happening in such close succession was a top-tier encounter.

After seeing nothing behind her, Jodie glanced down at her phone and realised she should be trying to communicate with the spirit to record any answers. Even if she didn't hear a reply, there was a chance her phone might pick something up her ears could not.

'Who are you?' she asked the empty space. 'Can you tell me?'

Nothing.

She continued to stare ahead into the darkness, not even able to see the far wall thanks to the curtains blocking any possible moonlight from seeping into the space.

Despite the eeriness, the utter darkness was a good thing. Jodie had no idea why, but it had always been true that settings with darkness and silence—even stillness—provided the most activity during investigations. Of course, being plunged into darkness only even worsened her anxiety, but such was life.

'Are you a child?' Jodie asked. Still nothing. 'Can you show yourself to me, or do something to let me know you're here?'

Jodie slowly panned her phone around the room. It was too dark for the camera to pick much up, but she was hoping the microphone might capture something.

Then she heard a sliding sound and whipped her head around to the tall chest of drawers, just in time to see the remote control atop it fall to the floor.

Her body instinctively tensed. Despite the fear, there was an undeniable excitement mixed in as well, so Jodie tried to focus on that. Even if all the activity decided to cease right then and there, this off-the-cuff seance session she'd partaken in had delivered far beyond what she could have hoped. Jodie just prayed her camera had picked up the falling remote.

'So... the remote control for the television just slid off that unit over there,' she whispered into her phone, providing commentary. She then slowly walked over and retrieved the remote, holding it closer to the camera for a second, before placing it back in its original spot. 'Can you do that again?' she asked.

Instead, there came an exhalation of breath from the opposite side of the room. Jodie whipped around, aiming her phone, fighting hard to stop from switching on her flashlight. 'H—hello?' She took a slow step forward. 'Is... is someone there?'

Despite moving closer, her viewfinder showed nothing, even when she was eventually able to pick up the far corner of the room.

'She's... noticed... you,' a small, wheezy voice suddenly said.

It came from behind Jodie, who spun again, drawing in a sharp breath, her body locked up with fear. However, there was still no one there.

Jodie was *certain* it had been a child's voice.

Keep calm, she ordered herself. *'She's noticed you?'* Jodie had no idea who *she* was. She quickly ran through what she knew of the reported hauntings at the Manor House; the only spirits documented were that of a young boy who had died of polio in the building, and that of a spiteful man named Robert Turner, a former owner who had been well-known and disliked in the town in the eighteen-hundreds.

As far as Jodie was aware, there were no female entities inhabiting the place.

'*Who* noticed me?' Jodie asked aloud. She waited for a response, but it didn't come. 'Hello? Can you tell me what you mean? I don't understand.'

Yet again, she was met only with silence.

After trying a few more times, it soon became apparent that the connection had been broken. Whatever spirit had been there was gone.

She felt a pang of disappointment at that, but at the same time, Jodie was elated at the things she'd experienced. She quickly got up and headed to the door to tell Tony everything, still thinking about what the spirit had said.

'She's... noticed... you.'

3

'Wow,' Tony exclaimed as they both stood out in the hallway, listening to the recording. 'I can definitely make out the voice. The remote falling from the cabinet is harder to see, since it's too dark, but that voice... that's fantastic evidence!' The man had a broad smile plastered across his face, his obvious excitement matching Jodie's.

'Not bad for a night's work, right?' Jodie asked as Tony handed her back the phone.

'Not bad at all,' he confirmed. 'Would you mind sending me a copy of the footage when you have a second? I'll run it through some software and increase the contrast, see if that shows anything else. I might try to tidy up the sound as well.'

'Sure,' she said. 'Are we gonna put it up on the website?'

'Of course. I mean, some of the people that attended tonight might be a little bummed it happened after they left, but this is good stuff. It'll certainly drum up interest for future events.'

As they moved back downstairs, Jodie realised the exhaustion she had previously felt was now gone—adrenaline continued to course through her. She hoped that it would subside soon, as the idea of facing the next day with absolutely *no* sleep was not an appealing one. But it was always the same after successful investigations: they gave her a rush that took a while to completely pass.

Once outside, Tony walked Jodie to her car, just as he always did. 'You have any plans for tomorrow?' he asked her.

'You mean today?' Jodie replied with a grin. 'It's after midnight.'

Tony laughed. 'Okay, any plans later today? It's Saturday. Surely you have something lined up,' he said as he opened the door to her hatchback for her.

'I'll probably go see my mum for a little bit,' Jodie said.

He nodded. 'How's she doing?'

'Not great,' Jodie replied with a shrug. 'She doesn't really remember me at all now.'

'Seeing her like that must be tough.'

'It's awful,' she said. 'But I go as often as I can. I don't like being there, but I do like being there *for her,* if that makes sense.'

'That makes perfect sense,' the man replied. 'And what about Sunday? Just a lazy day, or any plans?'

'Probably just a lazy day,' Jodie lied. 'What about you?'

'My eldest is coming over with his wife and the grandkids to see Alice and I, so we're both looking forward to that.'

'That's great,' Jodie said. She knew Tony's eldest son lived down in London, so Tony didn't get to see his grandchildren a whole lot.

'Yeah,' Tony replied with a big smile. 'And Carl, the oldest boy, *loves* that I hunt ghosts. He's only ten, but always asks me about it.'

'You gonna play him the video we just got? Let him hear that voice?'

Tony chuckled, but shook his head. 'That I don't know about. I'm careful what exactly I tell him. I don't want to give him sleepless nights. Plus, his mum doesn't like it when I share too much about what I do, which I understand.'

'Yeah, you don't want to scare the kid every time he comes up. I have a feeling the visits would get even less frequent that way.'

'Exactly,' Tony said. 'Come on, go get yourself home and get some sleep. And send me a text when—'

'When I get home,' Jodie finished. 'I'm fine, you know, Tony. You don't have to feel the need to look after me all the time.'

'It's late and you're driving alone. I just like to know you get back okay.'

'And how do I know when *you* get back okay?'

He laughed. 'Because I always reply when you tell me you're fine. Now stop arguing and go get some sleep.'

'Okay, will do.' Jodie got into the car and buckled up. Tony closed the door for her, tapped on the roof, then waved her off.

As she was slowly driving away, Jodie checked her rearview mirror to see Tony getting into his own SUV. She always joked that he didn't have to watch out for her, but in truth… she liked it. With both Mark and her father no longer around, it was nice knowing there was someone there for her if she needed them.

The drive back home took around twenty minutes, the roads quiet—so quiet she didn't see a single other vehicle on her way back to her small terrace home.

The house had been a starter home for her and Mark, and the idea had been to stay there for around five years while they saved for something better. But, of course, fate had had other ideas. A brain aneurysm had ruined all the dreams the couple had. Mark had been there one moment, literally gone the next, leaving behind a lifeless husk in the bed next to the sleeping Jodie, ready for her to find the next morning.

The street Jodie lived on was long, with terrace houses on either side of the road, some of the houses stepped to cope with the incline across the length of the street. She lived midway down, and as always, it was a squeeze to reverse park her vehicle into the spot just outside her house.

She got out, and then started to unload the equipment inside, dumping everything into the modest living room for the time being with the intention of putting it away properly after she'd slept. Once the car was unloaded, she came through to the kitchen, enjoying the silence the early hours of the morning offered. Jodie couldn't stop thinking about the events from earlier, and as she filled herself a glass of water, she took out her phone.

She was about to play back the footage when she decided instead to email the video file over to Tony first. As it was sending, she decided to pay a quick visit to the toilet to silence her complaining bladder. When she returned, she had a message from Tony already waiting for her.

Have you actually watched this all yet???

Jodie frowned, then tapped out: - *Briefly, with you. Why?* -

She then quickly opened the video, but before she could press play, a reply came back.

Watch it! But make sure to have the contrast up all the way. That's important.

Jodie raised an eyebrow as she opened the video in an editing app she had, whacked the contrast up to full, then set the video to play, watching with interest.

Because room six had been so dark at the time, it was difficult to make anything out, so the contrast only served to lighten what was in the immediate vicinity. She was able to see some of the bed and just barely glimpse the remote drop from the drawers. She kept watching.

Soon, Jodie heard the faint exhale through the recording, followed by her own gasp. The view on screen then moved around the bed and over to the far corner of the room, where the breath had come from.

Jodie quickly hit pause. Her mouth hung open, the hairs on the back of her neck standing up. 'What the hell?'

She stared wide-eyed at the frozen image on screen... where there was a boy.

He was sitting down, knees bent and arms wrapped around his legs as his head faced the camera, eyes glinting. While the image wasn't particularly clear, and still shrouded mostly in shadow despite the contrast adjustment, what Jodie was seeing was undeniable.

Jesus Christ!

Jodie pressed play again while holding her breath.

However, the moment the camera drew closer, the boy disappeared, seemingly swallowed up by the dark. She then heard the voice, weak and wheezy, utter: *'She's... noticed... you.'*

Jodie couldn't believe it. She quickly restarted the video and let the footage play out once more, pausing as the boy showed up, those glinting eyes searing into her. It might have only been for a few frames, but she realised the footage she was looking at was the singular best piece of evidence *Spirit Hunters* had ever gotten over their many years of investigations.

Oh. My. God!

She also realised that the ghostly boy had been in the room with her the entire time, even if he had remained unseen. And at *that* thought, Jodie couldn't help but shiver.

She typed out a message back to Tony: *The boy! This is unreal. I had no clue he was there!*

She saw the three dots appear on her screen, and the message soon came through: *You okay to take a call?*

Yeah!

No sooner had she sent her message than the call came in, which she immediately answered.

'Can you believe it?' she exclaimed without preamble.

'This is huge,' Tony said. 'That's a full apparition, Jodie. I know it doesn't stay there for long, but still.'

'It's unreal! Like I said in the text, I didn't see him with my own eyes when I was in the room.'

'Well, I figured you would have told me if you did,' Tony said with a chuckle.

'It's *contact*,' Jodie went on. 'Actual contact. He gave me a message and was looking right at me specifically. That means it isn't just a residual presence. I think there's intelligence there.' She didn't need to tell Tony how rare instances of genuine interaction or intelligence was with these entities.

'I agree,' he said. 'Which ties in with the story of the owner's son being thrown out of bed by something. That kind of thing doesn't happen in residual hauntings either.' He paused for a moment. 'I… I just can't believe it. We've never had anything even approaching this level of proof.'

Jodie heard the giddy excitement in her friend's voice and she couldn't help but smile.

'We need to share this on the website,' she said.

'Absolutely. I'm going to download it to my computer now, double save it to an external hard drive, and also upload it to our cloud. I don't want there to be any chance this thing goes missing. I'll update the website tomorrow.'

'It doesn't need to be *that* soon,' Jodie said. 'Your grand-kids are coming over, remember?'

'I… oh, yeah. Well, maybe Monday, then. But you know we'll need to be ready for the detractors to come out in force.'

Jodie hadn't even considered that, but she knew Tony was right. Whenever they'd posted evidence of activity over the years, a subset of people online had crawled out of the wood-work to cry 'fake.' And it wasn't just atheists or non-believers —she'd found other paranormal research companies would go out of their way to sabotage the competition in any way they could.

'Let them try to deny it,' Jodie said defiantly. 'The footage speaks for itself.'

'Well, to me and you it does,' Tony answered. 'But there'll still be those that say we used editing software or something.'

Jodie paused, then shrugged. 'Let them,' she repeated. 'We know it's true, and that means more than anything they might say against us.'

'Yeah,' Tony replied. 'Yeah... that's absolutely right. And you did good. *Really* good. It's amazing.'

'Oh, I was just in the room at the right time,' she said. 'I didn't do anything special. But seriously, just make sure you don't show it to your grandson! It made the hairs on *my* neck stand up, so he'd probably wind up having nightmares for weeks.'

'He's not going to see even a frame of this, don't worry,' Tony said. 'His mum would kill me, and that's assuming Alice didn't get to me first.' The two shared a laugh before Tony continued, 'Alright, well, I'll let you go get some sleep. I just wanted to call to... I don't know... share the excitement.'

'Yeah, I get it,' Jodie said. 'Sleep well.'

After hanging up, she let herself watch the video again a few more times. Each time she did, she couldn't help but shudder whenever she saw the boy's form. He was ghostly pale and had light-coloured shaggy hair, though it was hard to determine an exact colour on the video—it could have been blonde or even white. However, it was the glinting eyes that stuck with Jodie the most, even after she turned off the footage.

His words still swirled in her mind. She wasn't sure if it was a message, or maybe a warning. *Who* was watching her?

After finally going to bed, it took Jodie a frustratingly long time to drop off. The excitement she'd felt earlier had been reinvigorated after Tony's call, so it took far too long for her to calm down enough to feel sleepy. While she waited for unconsciousness to take her, she thought of the boy, but she also looked ahead at what she had planned on Sunday night—which was certainly *not* going to be a lazy day like she'd told Tony.

As much as Tony would no doubt freak out, the success of the Manor House made her more determined than ever to sneak into Parson Hall while she still had the chance. And in doing so, maybe she could ride this fresh wave of luck and get some evidence even more spectacular.

4

The common area of the old-folks home was spacious, with many elderly people seated inside. Some were talking to each other or to the visitors that had come to see them, some were watching the television in the corner, and others were simply staring into the void, with little signs of life behind their eyes.

At the moment, Jodie was sitting in a high-backed chair, the thin padding making the chair uncomfortable. She was positioned in the middle of a semi-circle of seats, which all faced the large television that played an old movie. Jodie's mother, Helen, was in the seat beside her, watching the television as well.

Her mother looked every inch of her eighty-two years: heavily lined face, thin grey hair, her body frail and hands curled from arthritis. Jodie, at thirty-eight, only carried a few lines of age around the sides of her mouth. She had inherited her mother's hazel eyes and high cheekbones, as well as a mouth that Jodie felt was a little too wide for her face.

Jodie had come along late in her parents' marriage, while both were in their forties, and it had affected Jodie growing up, having folks older than that of her friends. Now, she knew she was on the verge of saying goodbye to the last remaining parent. Helen's condition was constantly worsening, and Jodie didn't know how long her mother had left.

Jodie had arrived at the care home a little while ago, Helen had greeted her politely, but it was clear there had been no recognition in the older woman's eyes. And so they just sat without talking, watching the movie together. While it still broke Jodie's heart a little, it had been expected. It had been months since her own mother had truly recognised her.

'Do you like this one?' Jodie eventually asked, leaning closer to her mum. 'The movie, I mean.'

Her mother gave Jodie a polite smile. It was one Jodie had seen over the years, which Helen always gave to strangers. It felt like a small stab to the heart.

'It passes the time,' Helen said. 'I'd prefer to be reading, though. I always liked my books. Haven't the foggiest idea where mine have gone now.'

'Would you like me to bring you some new ones? I can do that next time I come in.'

'Oh, my dear, a young pretty thing like you shouldn't concern yourself with me. I'm sure you have a full life to live, rather than spending time with strangers.'

Stab.

'It's me, Mum,' Jodie patiently said. 'Jodie, your daughter.'

She saw her mother turn to her and cast Jodie a confused frown. There was a flicker of something on her face—maybe recognition—but it was all too brief, quickly replaced by that polite smile again. 'Now that I'm thinking about it, some books *would* be appreciated.'

'I'll bring you some in,' Jodie said. 'Don't worry, I know the kind of stories you like.'

'Well thank you. Do you like reading, dear?'

Jodie nodded. 'I do, yes.'

'Let me guess, you love a nice romantic story, eh?'

Jodie chuckled. 'Actually, I prefer ghost stories.'

She saw Helen give an exaggerated shudder. 'You shouldn't read that kind of thing. It's not good for the soul.'

'Eh, I enjoy them,' Jodie replied. 'They can be scary, but it's just like going on a roller coaster, getting that thrill, you know?'

But Helen shook her head. 'No, it isn't like that at all.' The woman then leaned in. 'There are things people shouldn't mess around with,' she whispered in a conspiratorial tone. '*Real* things. My own mother, God rest her soul, had an interest in that kind of thing as well. Terrible business. It ended up putting my daughter in danger.' Helen hesitated. 'I've never been able to forgive Mum for that.'

Jodie raised her eyebrows in surprise. In all the years since the events at her grandmother's house, she had never been sure just *how* much her mother knew. Jodie had obviously told Helen everything that she'd witnessed, but she'd always gotten the impression her mother had downplayed many of Jodie's claims, which made Jodie believe Helen simply hadn't believed her. And Jodie hadn't known if her mother had spoken to Grandma about it in the short time her grandmother had been around following the events.

Jodie wondered if she could pry a little more info from Helen now. Over the last few weeks, Helen's long-term memory had seemed to come back in brief waves, and when it did, she often divulged a lot, usually unprompted.

'That sounds awful,' Jodie said, trying to continue the conversation.

Helen nodded. 'I thought what happened would have made my Jodie too terrified to ever talk about ghosts and things like that again. But...' Helen sighed. 'She started to take an interest. Still does. She's in college, but I know she is obsessed. I suppose it's natural. I guess she's still trying to come to terms with it all.'

'College, huh?' Jodie asked.

Helen nodded. 'Yes.' A huge smile then spread over her face. 'She's very bright.'

'And... did your daughter tell you what happened that night? With your mother?'

Helen's smile fell away. 'She did.'

'And you believed her?'

A nod. 'Of course. Though I tried to brush it off as much as I could. To protect her, you know?'

'I... understand,' Jodie said, hiding the wave of emotion that rolled over her. *All these years of thinking she never believed me...* 'I'm sure she'd understand,' Jodie said.

'Anyway, I don't like talking about it.' Helen crossed her arms and sunk back into her chair.

Jodie wasn't about to give up, however—she wanted to know more.

'I'm a good listener,' she prodded. 'If you want to talk about it, feel free to tell me.'

Helen shook her head. 'No, dear, I don't want to burden you with it. I... can't even remember why we started talking about it. Do... do you know my Jodie? You have a look of her.'

'I... no, I don't know her,' Jodie said. Normally on her visits, she'd gently remind her mother just who she was, in the hopes it would spark recognition, but she held off this time, not wanting to agitate the woman. 'She sounds nice, though.'

'She is!' Helen said, her smile returning, full of pride. 'She's courteous, caring, but... she has an independent streak too.' Helen's smile widened, clearly remembering something. 'When she sets her mind to something it's impossible to deter her. The amount of times she snuck out at night to meet her friends when she was in school... it drove me up the wall. But she kept doing it, no matter how much I scolded her. Staying out late, going to parties. I remember her and her friends broke into an old building one night so they could all get drunk.'

Jodie repressed a smile, knowing her mother didn't know the half of it. She also thought of her upcoming excursion to Parson Hall. *Some things never change.*

'I'm sure she didn't mean to get you so angry,' Jodie said.

'Oh, I know she didn't. She just has a lot of character and knows her own mind. A lot like her dad.' Helen leaned her head back in the chair and let her eyes gaze around the room. 'Ugh. I do hate coming here. This room. This place. It feels like... like everyone is on their last stop on the way to nothing.' She looked at her sleek, silver watch: a gift from Jodie's dad. 'Still, my husband will be along shortly to collect me.'

Another stab.

'That's nice,' Jodie said. As she looked at her mother, she saw a glaze fall over the woman's eyes, the sparkle of intelligence dulling in an instant. Helen slowly turned to her.

'Who... who are you?'

'I...' Jodie started, but then trailed off. 'We've been talking just now. Don't you remember?'

A confused frown crossed Helen's face. She shook her head. 'N—no.'

Jodie offered her a sympathetic, tight-lipped smile. 'That's fine. I'm just here keeping you company and watching television with you.'

Helen nodded as more of her sparkle slipped away. She didn't say anything else for the entire time Jodie was there.

After another hour, Jodie gave her mother a hug and a kiss—though the woman barely seemed to notice—then walked outside and got into her car. Once there, she allowed herself to cry.

5

THE REMAINDER OF JODIE'S WEEKEND—UP UNTIL SUNDAY night—had been uneventful. After feeling elated in the early hours of Saturday morning, still riding the high of the previous night, the visit to see her mother had instantly brought her back down to earth with a bump. The visits were always hard, but learning her mother had actually believed Jodie about the events of her youth had been something of a revelation she was still struggling to process. That, mixed with seeing her mother fade away again before her very eyes, had left Jodie uneasy and rudderless. She had more questions for her mother, yet she didn't know how much time she had left to ask them.

When evening hit, Jodie stood outside her house, looking into the open boot of her vehicle, mentally checking off everything she'd packed, making sure nothing had been forgotten.

She was dressed in her standard ghost hunting attire—or her uniform, as she called it: hiking boots with thick socks, jeans, t-shirt with a jumper over it, and a grey wool coat. She also wore a black wool hat over her long, dark hair. There was a lot of equipment in her car, and Jodie knew she probably wouldn't be able to use most of it given she might have to move quickly, but she'd rather be over prepared than under.

Then, upon realising she was actually going to go through with this, with *trespassing*, a nervous energy quickly hit her.

Am I actually going to do this?

She knew she was.

In the early days of investigating, she and Mark had received a few slaps on the wrists after being caught in places they shouldn't have been. It had never amounted to anything serious, and in truth she knew the same would likely apply here if she were caught. Plus, Jodie had driven past the property a few times over the last few weeks to scope it out, and knew the security cameras were now gone. Likely sold off to help cover the former owner's debt. And with the sale not finalised, English Heritage hadn't installed any new cameras or security fencing of their own.

The building was technically in limbo. A perfect opportunity.

She'd also taken tomorrow off from her marketing job in preparation, so another late night wouldn't be an issue. Everything was in place; everything was ready. *It'd be foolish to back out now.*

But she wondered what she would do if she captured evidence of any truly great phenomena, because… what could she do with it?

She couldn't tell Tony or show him—he'd be furious at her sneaking into places she shouldn't have been. Which meant she might have to keep her findings to herself.

In the end, though, Jodie was fine with that. The whole excursion was a personal pilgrimage, anyway.

Jodie returned to her house to set the alarm and lock the front door before getting into the driver's side of her vehicle.

Here we go.

Since it was ten o'clock, and she had a forty-minute drive ahead of her, she figured she'd be inside Parson Hall before eleven. Jodie had mentally allowed herself two or three hours at the location, and she just hoped she was brave enough to fully see them through. As she set off, her nerves started to grow, and the subdued energy she'd had for most of the day shifted to tension. Being alone in a haunted location was a far different prospect than being there with Tony.

Be brave. You can do it.

Just like the early hours of Saturday morning, the roads were quiet again, which was perfect. She let the radio play to itself, barely taking any notice of the generic pop song that played, concentrating instead at what lay before her. Eventually, she arrived in the small market borough of Framwelgate, which was in the same county she lived in—County Durham—but on the opposite side. Jodie had to pass through the borough's empty streets and make her way to the north side of the settlement. There she took a quiet country road leading northeast. The narrow road had tall trees dominating either side. Because of that, and because of the lack of street lighting, she had to drive slowly with full beam on her headlights. Fortunately, she didn't have to go far down that road before she hit the left-hand turnoff that led down to the hall. There had once been a metal gate at the entrance, stopping uninvited people from heading down. That was now gone, the iron probably sold off, leaving the entrance pillars standing bare.

This second road was even narrower than the previous one, but there were no trees flanking the way ahead. This *would* have exposed a vast expanse of fields on either side of her, had the whole area not been swallowed up by the night.

Thanks to the power of her headlights, she could now just make out the hall up ahead. Eventually, more trees came into view again closer to the building, circling around the structure. Another turnoff opened up to her immediate right, giving access to a fully paved area that had once served as a car park. Jodie ignored that and kept going closer to the building. She knew a little about the history of the hall. The oldest part had been built in the fourteenth century, with sandstone walls and pitched slate roofs running at different angles and giving an interesting architectural appeal. The main entrance was situated in the original building, where there were large Georgian windows on the ground and middle floors. A third storey was denoted by a smaller window set into a gable peak of the roof space.

To the right of the original structure was a brick addition that Jodie knew had been constructed in the eighteenth century. The elevations were rather plain: tall, rectangular, with three windows set uniformly along each of the stories. The pitched roof ran right-to-left across the front of the building.

The whole structure was a mesh of styles, and the wings on either side of the central connecting section were higher than the middle.

Jodie drove as close as she could, and pulled the car over, looking around the area to make sure there were no other vehicles. Thankfully, as far as she could tell, the coast was clear.

She got out of the car and stood beside it for a few moments, coat pulled tight, listening to the near silence around her, broken only by the chirping of insects. The building looked foreboding in the near-dark, and a familiar chill of anticipation ran up her spine; tonight it was more intense than usual, thanks to being alone. It was the first time she'd ever carried out an investigation solo in all her years of doing this.

Am I really going to go in there?

She'd asked herself that many times over the past week, as well as many times on the drive over. Every time, she'd known the answer deep down. Now, though... she wasn't as certain, and genuine doubts had started to take over.

Doubts born from fear.

It's not too late. I can just get in the car, turn around, and go home. No one would ever know I chickened out.

And she seriously considered it. It felt like the safer option, and in many ways, the *right* option.

But then she thought of Mark, of the passion they'd shared, of the special night they had together in Parson Hall. Their fear, their nervous laughter, then their shock and elation of him dropping to a knee and proposing—he'd been completely unprepared and hadn't even had a ring. It hadn't mattered to Jodie. Not one jot. The proposal had been raw and pure and honest.

Jodie realised she hadn't come to the hall to hunt ghosts. She'd come to relive a moment.

One of the happiest of her life.

With that in mind, she locked the car and set off walking to the main entrance.

She had to travel a hundred meters or so down a path towards the main entrance; wild grass and shrubs were overgrown on either side, sometimes coming up above waist-height, with the path forming a corridor through the greenery.

The gardens themselves, both to the front and back on the generous amount of land on the property, had once been a point of pride, something people came to see, irrespective of the hall itself. Those days were long gone now, and everything was wild and uncared for, with weeds rife throughout the whole area.

The occasional stone crunched under her hiking boots as she drew closer. On her walk, she searched her mind to summon what she could remember of the history of the building. She, Mark, and Tony had researched it prior to their investigation, so she felt she had a pretty good grounding of it, though maybe not as detailed as she'd have liked. But everything basically revolved around events that took place in the late eighteen hundreds, when one of the estate stewards had been found guilty of multiple murders. He'd avoided a court trial—since the local villagers had judged him and beaten him to death.

Nathaniel Barrow. The Watcher of Parson Hall.

So called because it had turned out he had a tendency for voyeurism. Nathaniel had come to see himself as something of a protector of Parson Hall, so the stories went, and his delusions had led to him killing people. Over the years, guests and owners of the hall had long reported feelings of being watched, shadowy figures, and hearing disembodied whispers and breathing.

Thinking about the reports and history associated with the building gave Jodie pause yet again.

I'm here now. I have *to keep going.*

But as she drew closer, Jodie knew she still had to find a way inside. The building was sure to be locked up tight. Even so, she had an idea. One Tony would have really lost his shit over.

I just hope the alarms aren't active.

Because if they were, she would need to make an extremely fast getaway. She just hoped what she'd heard about the power being cut off was true.

After steeling herself, she walked up to the main door: a thick wooden entrance door, single leaf, with an arched head and no glazed sections. It looked like something you might find in an old church. She tentatively tried the cast-iron handle and, as expected, found it locked via the deadbolt.

You didn't really expect to just waltz right in, Jodie, did you?

she asked herself. She hadn't, of course, but it would have been nice.

So... breaking and entering it was.

She figured the best place to do that was around the back, so Jodie set off walking the perimeter, pushing her way through the overgrown shrubbery that hung over the path. Once at the rear, she moved to the old hall. There was a back door there, but that was locked up tight as well, so she moved closer to one of the windows instead, which were tall and split into glazed, rectangular sections by Georgian bars. The panes of glass were about fifteen inches by twenty inches—far too small to fit through. However, that wasn't her plan. She looked around the ground and quickly found a suitably sized rock. With the rock in hand, she stood before the window and took a breath.

Am I really going to do this?

She'd done worse in her youth. *But I'm an adult now. A responsible adu—*

Jodie threw the rock.

Even though the shattering glass made an undeniably satisfying sound, her body tensed up. She waited with bated breath, expecting to hear the blaring of an alarm... but once the sound of smashing glass died out in the night, there was only silence.

Jodie exhaled. *Thank God.*

She did feel bad for having to break the window, but given how much of the building already looked like it needed repair, she was sure it wouldn't affect the new owners much. The windows themselves looked like replacements, so not originals that needed to be preserved.

You're just excusing your vandalism, she chastised herself. *Not cool.*

Pushing aside her guilt, Jodie wrapped her fist in the thick sleeve of her coat and batted away the remaining jagged glass to the lower area of the pane she'd broken. Once she determined it was safe, she reached her hand inside, now easily able to reach the latch. Jodie unlocked it and was able to lift up the sliding sash, finally giving her access.

Once done, she retrieved her flashlight from her deep coat pocket and flashed the beam inside the dark hall. She could see lots of brown and grey stone to the walls and floor, with the blocks to the wall all different sizes, and large square tiles on the floor. The ceiling was vaulted, the roof timbers all exposed. There was a brick fireplace to the far end built into one of the walls, but little else to see, other than the light fittings fixed to the beams. Jodie knew they wouldn't work, however; the lack of any alarm had proven her theory about the building having no power.

Jodie then leaned inside, pushing herself forward, before swinging a leg over the sill to awkwardly climb through and into the hall. Once inside, she stood back up and looked around. The silence was almost oppressive and the feeling of isolation heavy. For what felt like the tenth time that night, she had to fight against the idea of fleeing.

Calm down, she told herself. *No one is gonna know I was ever here.* She took a steadying breath. Then another thought struck her. *Maybe some*thing *knows you're here.*

She gazed around, the beam from her light panning across the hall that was roughly fifteen feet wide and thirty feet in length. Jodie coughed, not because she needed to, but more to see what it would sound like in the bare room. As expected, it echoed thanks to the lack of soft furnishings or carpet to dampen the sound. Up above, there was a mezzanine floor that ran out from the inner wall by a few feet and offered a balcony view of the hall.

Jodie debated whether she should spend a bit of time looking around first, or if she should go back to the car to grab her equipment and bring it inside. Getting a lay of the land would be a good idea, since she hadn't been here in years, but on the other hand, if something happened straight away, it would be good to have the equipment at the ready to capture it. After a moment's consideration, she decided to do a sweep. *I do have my phone, so I can use that to record if need be.* It wouldn't help with cold spots, and the microphone wasn't the best for audio, but it was something. *Definitely worked well back at the Manor House.*

As she moved, Jodie tried to keep her footsteps light. The heels on her boots were short, but still hard, and they clicked as she walked across the stone tiles.

After leaving the hall, Jodie found herself in the long entrance corridor, which had a small, closed lobby to the front. The floor there was lined with timber planks and the smooth plasterboard on the walls had been painted a pastel green. The ceiling was mostly flat, save for cornices around the edges and ceiling roses around the hanging light fittings. The corridor cut across the full depth of the building, running front to back; access to the rest of the building was via a door opposite the hall. That door led to a huge function space, and then from there one could get to the stairs to the upper floors, or carry on farther and reach the kitchen and living areas.

Jodie entered the function area and tried one of the light switches, just out of curiosity. Nothing.

The large space looked more modern than the almost-medieval-feeling original hall, with the same timber-plank flooring from the entrance corridor and flat ceiling with exposed cross beams. The walls were painted plaster—most a dull yellow, but the one housing a fireplace a striking purple. The far end of the space was raised, accessed by a short flight of steps the full width of the room, and there was a bar tucked into the corner at the top. The door to the stairwell was also up in that raised area to the back. There were some hard-back chairs close to Jodie that looked like they should have been accompanied by a dining-room table, but the table wasn't present. There was also a long, rectangular patterned rug, which Jodie guessed was where the table had once sat. Like the old hall, the function room felt bare—little more than a lingering memory, devoid of any former vibrancy of life.

Jodie decided to check out the far end of the ground floor first, so she walked through into a small lobby with a toilet accessed from it. Beyond the lobby there was another long corridor, one that had a bank of glazing across on both walls, looking out into the gardens. There wasn't much to see at that time of night, of course. At the end of the corridor were four doors: two on the left, one straight ahead, and one on the right. She took the first door on the left, entering a small sitting room with green-painted walls, patterned carpet on the floor, and some bench seating built into one of the walls. There was also a single circular table left in place. The next door on the left entered into a drawing room, which was about double the size of the sitting room. Here, the walls were panelled and painted a dull yellow, and some dusty sofas remained in place, a few covered by cloth. The floor consisted of wooden planks again, though this time with a dark oak stain.

The door to the far end of the corridor gave access to a living room with a small kitchenette space attached, though only the cupboards remained in the kitchenette, with all appliances now stripped out. This space felt modern, with magnolia walls and the ash-wood floor. There were spotlights on the flat ceiling.

There was also a door at the back of the room, opening to a small utility room, where there was a large stainless-steel sink but little else.

Back out into the corridor, Jodie took the last remaining

door, which opened into a second stairwell leading to the next floor up.

Before taking the stairs, however, she hesitated. The space was incredibly dark; there were a few windows higher up above her, but they didn't allow much moonlight to seep in. The timber stairs that ran up to a half-landing and turned back on themselves looked particularly foreboding. The wing of the building she was in currently operated as the main space guests stayed in, given it could be easily closed off from the corridor and left-hand wing, becoming its own little self-contained space.

She thought about going up, wanting to see how much had changed since her last time at the hall. Of course, the primary room she wanted to check was the attic. Well, saying she *wanted* to go there wasn't quite true. It was the place she was most afraid of.

Just check out the living quarters for now, Jodie told herself. *Save the other wing for later, hopefully I'm feeling braver then.*

She again thought of going back to the car for the equipment, but pushed on and moved up to the next floor, her footfalls echoing again, this time louder against the wooden treads of the stairs. Upstairs there was another sitting room, a bedroom and en-suite, and then another corridor like the one below, running across to the other wing. There was also a third floor to her current wing, utilising the same staircase. When Jodie headed up she found a living area and bedroom, which were both repeats of the one on the middle floor, only with a larger en-suite and storage cupboard opposite in the bedroom. There was no corridor here to the far wing, however. *No way to get across.*

Like the other rooms, the bedrooms were bare, with no beds left behind and not much in the way of furniture—the top story bedroom had an old wardrobe, which was empty, and a single hard-backed seat, that had been dropped off strangely in the centre of the room, right below a hanging light fitting. While in the top bedroom, Jodie looked out over the grounds, seeing the lights from the nearby town. The settlement was only a ten-minute drive away, but her being all alone in the empty, abandoned house made it seem like civilisation was as far away as the moon.

Don't spook yourself.

Jodie felt like she was giving herself a lot of these little pep-talks. Fear was understandable, but she had known what she was getting into, so she was a little disappointed in herself for constantly being so unnerved.

Nothing here can hurt you. Just finish looking around, then go back to the car.

After heading down to the mid floor again, Jodie moved along the corridor to access the opposite wing, where she found a room to her left that looked to have been a small bedroom, and then a larger interconnecting room straight ahead. This larger space was bare again, and it would have given no indication to its former function had it not been for the en-suite close to her. The second exit from the room came out in a small hallway in the far wing. It was strange having to go through a room to access that side of the building, but she'd been in many old buildings with strange layouts over the years. The small hallway she was now in housed the stairs back down to the ground floor, as well as a door that opened out to the balcony above the old hall. There was also another door that gave access to a narrow flight of stairs, which ran up to the attic.

Jodie didn't go up, and just stared at the closed door for a moment, then finally ignored it and instead moved out into the mezzanine floor to the old hall, using her flashlight to peer down to the dark space below. In its prime, the building had been a venue for small weddings, and the hall no doubt held many happy memories for people, filled with laughter and music and dancing.

She was struck with a feeling of melancholy, staring down and remembering how Mark had dropped to his knee in that very room, much to the shock of her and Tony. It had taken her less than a second to yell out, 'I do!' and throw her arms around him—she'd clearly felt his racing heart against her chest as she'd hugged him.

After a few moments, Jodie turned and walked back towards the door to the small hallway.

Clomp, clomp, clomp.

Jodie froze, her body growing tight, heart seizing at the distinct footsteps down below. She quickly spun and tentatively moved over to the balcony handrail, aiming her flashlight beam into the hall a level lower once more.

The footsteps had come from there, clear as day, sounding like someone was moving from the back of the room towards the front. Thanks to her shaking hand, the light from her flashlight was unsteady.

There was no doubt in her mind as to what she'd heard, no way it could have been something explainable. The footsteps had been too clear.

Jodie waited, breath held, staring down into the sea of darkness that was broken only by the spear of light from her flashlight. She moved the beam around like a spotlight, searching for the cause of the sound, expecting to see a figure or shadow.

There was nothing.

She drew out her phone and started to record video and audio. *Maybe I'll get lucky again, like I did at the Manor House.* But after standing and scanning the area for a little while more, Jodie had to accept that the brief phenomena was over. Even so, it had left her on edge, with a feeling of creeping dread crawling over her.

I need my equipment, she realised. If she'd had an experience already, not even a half hour after arriving, then it could end up being an eventful night. She wanted to get as much evidence as she possibly could—for her own collection, if nothing else.

But that didn't matter. Even if it *was* just for her, that would be good enough. Just more proof that there was life after death. More proof that Mark still existed out there somewhere.

And maybe there will be a way to see him again one day, just to tell him one more time how much I love him. How much he changed my life.

Jodie put her phone away, turned, and moved back out of the hall, once again entering the small hallway. Her attention was immediately drawn to the attic door again.

It was open.

Only a crack, but it was enough, and Jodie was certain it had been closed before. She tried to think logically, to make sure she wasn't jumping to any conclusions. *Was there a draft?* Not that she'd noticed. *Was the door* really *all the way closed before?* She… thought so. She was almost sure of it.

Almost.

She froze as the door then slowly drifted open before her eyes with a creak.

Oh God!

Eventually, the door stopped, hanging ninety degrees open. The darkness beyond was thick and heavy, like a sea of black. With a shaking hand, Jodie held her flashlight up to let the beam reach farther, which allowed her to see the start of the stairs, though nothing was there.

Jodie was rooted to the spot, eyes wide, her breathing growing faster and faster.

Keep control. You're used to these things.

While that was true enough, she wasn't used to dealing with them alone.

She continued to stare, waiting, just gazing into the yawning black. The shadows were almost taunting her, as if daring someone to enter. Jodie wondered if the door opening was some kind of invitation for her to go up.

Maybe this place... remembers me from before?

But Jodie couldn't move. It was as if her feet were made of lead. And that was made worse by a sinking feeling in her gut, one that told her going up to the attic would be a *very* bad idea.

Jodie instead took half a step back, eyes firmly fixed on the open doorway. She was staring so intently, the shadows started to move. It was a trick of the mind, she had no doubt about that, the way someone's vision could cause objects to shift if they stared long and hard enough, yet it still didn't stop her mind kicking into overdrive, imagining a pale hand reaching out or a decomposed face slowly leaning out of the shadows as it stared at her.

Stop it!

Jodie forced her mind to remain in the present and focus on what was real, stopping her imagination from running away with itself.

Thud.

Jodie gasped and quickly shifted backwards. It hadn't been a footstep, far too heavy for that, sounding instead like something heavy had fallen over in the attic.

This was a mistake. Coming here at all was a mistake, she thought. *I need to run.*

She battled with the idea. She had her reasons for being at Parson Hall, but even that had just been a vague hope. She knew it was unlikely the visit would really bring her any peace. In truth, experiencing paranormal activity had been of secondary importance. Now that it was happening, however, while she was all alone, it made Jodie realise just how stupid the whole idea had been. Besides, she had seen the old hall again, the spot where Mark had proposed, and briefly relived the moment. Maybe that was enough. Maybe her true mission had been accomplished.

Time to go.

After summoning all of her remaining strength, Jodie turned and quickly walked away through the interconnecting bedroom and then out to the corridor again. In truth, it would have been faster to take the flight of stairs in the short hallway behind her, but that meant going past the open attic door, and the idea of doing that was just too much. So instead, Jodie jogged down the corridor to the far wing, constantly looking back over her shoulder, expecting to see something rushing out of the darkness towards her, arms outstretched.

As she moved, her attention was drawn to yet another sound. This one wasn't inside the house, however, and it certainly wasn't paranormal.

Jodie stopped as soon as she reached the bank of glazing that looked out over the front of the property. There she saw it: a pair of headlights coming down the narrow road towards the house. The sound was that of a rumbling engine getting louder as the vehicle drew closer.

What the hell?

Jodie's heart sank even more. Realisation drew over her. She wasn't sure how, but it was clear *someone* knew she was at the property.

And she was about to be caught red-handed.

6

Oh shit, oh shit, oh shit.

Jodie's mind tried to figure out just *how* someone knew she was there. She wondered if she had been spotted driving towards the property, or maybe an alarm *was* active.

Ultimately, she realised the reason was irrelevant. It was happening, and she needed to deal with it. She then tried to think of a way she could escape before being found. But getting back to her car undetected would be difficult, if not impossible—she wouldn't be able to drive away without being spotted. In fact, she knew her car was likely to be seen as soon as the approaching vehicle got closer. If the person investigating had any sense, they would no doubt grab her licence plate. That way, even if she *did* manage to get clear, a quick trace would link the break-in straight back to her.

I'm screwed.

She imagined how upset and disappointed Tony was going to be. He was proud of the reputation they'd built for *Spirit Hunters,* yet her actions tonight might well have jeopardised all that. She imagined how gleefully rival organisations would spread the news on social media, highlighting how *Spirit Hunters* had a criminal as co-owner.

Shit, shit, shit.

Even so, she still needed to decide what she was going to do. She watched the vehicle draw closer, which was a large, black SUV. It slowed down near her own vehicle, then stopped in the road for a few moments, before finally reversing to tuck itself in to the verge, parking just behind Jodie's car.

It hadn't blocked her in, but given the roadway was so tight, turning her vehicle around and inching past the new car would be a squeeze. Any residual thoughts of a quick, sneaky getaway vanished completely.

Just face up to it, she told herself with heavy reassignment. *Go out there and own up. See if you can charm your way through it.* It would be a tough ask. Simply batting her eyelashes wasn't likely to be enough to excuse breaking into a building, but she hoped she could resolve it without getting the law involved. She would just say the building meant a lot to her and she'd wanted to look around it alone one last time while she still could. She'd admit to breaking the window, offer to pay, and throw herself at their mercy.

She glanced back down the hallway again, still feeling uneasy about what she'd heard from the attic. The tiny silver lining from someone showing up was that at least she wasn't alone anymore.

Time to face the music, she told herself, knowing there was no point in putting it off.

Just as she was about to set off, she saw the SUV door open and a tall figure get out. She couldn't make out too much, but Jodie was sure it was a man, and he looked to be a few inches over six feet tall. He was dressed in a thick coat that made it difficult to see how broad he was.

Security of some kind?

Jodie started to move, happy to get farther away from the attic, and headed down to the ground floor. There, she started towards the old hall, and when she entered the main corridor, she saw the searching light from a flashlight penetrate the windows. Jodie was still out of sight, to the side of the windows, her own flashlight now off so as not to draw attention. She pushed her head closer to the glass, peeking out. The stranger was close now, which let Jodie hear his footsteps moving to the front door. Nervousness gripped her.

She heard him shake the door handle, though more to test the lock.

Jodie contemplated calling out, just so he knew there was someone inside—at least that way he'd know no one was hiding in the shadows. It might help defuse a potentially volatile situation.

However, Jodie waited, apprehensive, suddenly aware this person might *not* be simply checking on the property.

Maybe they were there for similar reasons: to look around while the place was empty. Maybe it was someone that needed shelter and had been using the abandoned place. Then again, if someone needed an abandoned building to rest their heads, she doubted they would be driving such a nice SUV.

She listened intently at the sound of slow footsteps as the man started to walk the perimeter, realising he'd soon get to the window she'd opened. Jodie debated running back to close it, though she also considered opening one to the front while he was at the rear, then sprinting over to her car to lock herself inside. The man would hear as soon as she started the engine, of course. *And he'd probably get to me before I even turned the car around. Though maybe I could speak to him from inside. At least that way I'd be safe.*

Her gut told her something was off about the whole situation. Unless a secret alarm had alerted the man, then it didn't make sense he was there. *If he's security of some kind, shouldn't he be calling out and asking who's here?*

Jodie decided to wait a few moments, making up her mind in that instant to flee back to her car when the moment was right. Her heart continued to race, and she cursed herself for getting into such a stupid—and avoidable—situation.

Yet a few seconds later, as Jodie was still trying to decide which window to open, she realised she couldn't hear the man anymore. *Did he stop moving?*

She listened intently. After a few moments, she heard him walking again, quietly, heading back the way he'd come. Jodie pressed herself against the glass, trying to see the corner of the building. His light soon came into view, so she ducked down; a second later the man appeared as well, walking along the front length of the building, drawing closer to her.

The beam of light swung left and right on his approach. Jodie knew she needed to move. However, just as she pulled back, the light flicked over and settled on her just before she pulled out of sight. *Damn it, was I quick enough?*

'Someone in there?' a gruff, strong voice called.

Jodie hesitated, again cursing herself. She let out a sigh, knowing she couldn't hide anymore.

'Yeah,' she called back, then followed up with: 'who are you?' Jodie tried adding steel to her voice, an assertive edge, to hopefully make it sound like she had every reason to be there. If the man was trespassing as well, maybe her tone would be enough to put him off and leave.

The reply that came avoided her question all together. 'What are you doing here?' the man shouted.

Jodie clenched her teeth. 'I'm supposed to be here,' she lied, taking a chance. 'What are *you* doing here?'

There was a moment's pause. 'You're lying.'

'Am I?'

'The front and back doors are locked up,' he called. 'I can see into the hall from here. A window is open and some of the glass is smashed.'

Shit.

'It was like this when I got here.'

'And you just… crawled in through the open window to check it all out?'

Shit, shit. Jodie paused. 'Yes.'

'If you're supposed to be here, why didn't you use a key?'

Another pause, but then Jodie shouted back: 'Why don't *you?*'

There was no reply. Everything fell quiet. *No…* She heard something faint. Jodie leaned closer to the window again and saw the flashlight move once more, accompanying the sound of light footsteps. He was sneaking closer.

Jodie's heartrate increased. The windows in the corridor didn't open, which meant she had to go back to either the hall to escape, or continue to the living quarters.

Just as the man stepped in front of the window, almost blinding her with his light, Jodie bolted towards the living quarters. She heard him run as well, sprinting past the window, so she halted, heart hammering in her chest. It was clear he was aiming to head her off, so she spun and ran back the other way. She heard his footfalls stop, turn, and head back, running at a furious pace—he'd obviously figured out her tactic. Regardless, Jodie kept going, running as fast as she could, losing sight of him as she cut through the function space, out to the entrance corridor, and into the main hall.

She stopped dead.

He was climbing through the window. She still couldn't make much out, dazzled by the flashlight beam that fell on her.

'Wait!' he shouted. 'I need to talk to you.'

She didn't answer and ran, her feet pounding as she made her way back across the building, hearing him follow quickly behind. She burst through into the sitting room and raced over to one of the windows. The man's heavy, thudding footsteps drew ever closer.

Jodie tried to twist open the window latch… but the mechanism wouldn't budge.

She tried again, harder this time, her fingers blooming with pain as she gripped the metal clasp. It was no good. The latch had become fused in place through lack of use over the years.

Shit.

She moved to the next window, but just as she reached it, the beam from the man's torch flooded the room, catching Jodie square in the face.

'Wait!' the man ordered, face still hidden behind his light. Jodie held a hand up before her face, squinting, adrenaline racing through her body.

'Get that light out of my face,' she snapped back, teeth clenched.

To her surprise, the man listened, lowering his flashlight.

'Sorry,' he said.

Motes swam in Jodie's vision. She blinked a few times to try to bring things into focus. Eventually, she looked over at the stranger, who seemed happy enough standing in the doorway and blocking her escape.

Given the light was no longer blinding her, it helped Jodie take in his details. She guessed he was in his early thirties and he had a gaunt, weathered face with patchy stubble and scraggly brown hair. His thin lips were pressed together; Jodie also noticed his creased forehead, emblematic of someone that spent much of their life frowning.

The stranger wore a pea-green, fur-trimmed-hood coat,

combat trousers, and walking boots. The only thing in his hands was the torch.

'Who are you?' Jodie demanded.

He slowly shook his head. 'You first. And also, why are you here?' There was a distinctly threatening tone to his words.

Jodie made a small sidestep towards the next window, keeping her eyes firmly on him. 'I'm *supposed* to be here,' she lied again. It was pointless, clear as day she was bluffing, but she clung to it anyway because one thing was for certain: *he* sure as shit wasn't supposed to be there either.

'Can you stop with the bullshit?' the man said as he shook his head.

'Can *you?*' she shot back. 'Just tell me who you are. You're clearly not here to check up on the place.'

'I am, I'm security,' he said.

'Now who's talking bullshit?'

'I *am* supposed to be here,' he replied, trying to sound sincere but failing drastically. Instead, he just sounded... tired. 'I check up on this place once or twice a night,' he went on. 'Drove down and saw your car. Then saw what you did to the window.'

Jodie hesitated. Her gut told her not to believe him, though she knew it technically *could* be true. He had a certain air about him that made him a good fit for security, maybe former military or that kind of thing. Regardless, something didn't fit.

'I don't believe you,' she said. 'But... whatever. It doesn't matter. I'm leaving now anyway.' She took another step towards the window.

'That would be a good move,' the man said.

Jodie paused. 'You... aren't going to stop me?'

He shook his head, grey eyes focused on her intently. 'No. I think it's best if you go, then I can fix up everything here.'

Jodie cocked her head to the side. 'Normally, if security found someone breaking into a building, they'd want the perpetrator arrested.'

'So you *did* break in,' he said. Jodie just held eye contact with the man, who shrugged. 'Look, I don't need the hassle of calling the police and going through everything with them, only for you to just get a slap on the wrist. None of it is worth it. Just go home.'

'And you don't want to know what I'm doing here?'

'Don't much care,' the man said. 'It's not like you're stealing stuff—there isn't anything of value here. So I'm guessing you just had an interest in the building and wanted to check it out.'

'And I can just drive away, no questions asked?'

'Yes,' the man said. 'But if you hang around, then I *am* calling the police and we'll go through the whole ordeal. But I'd rather not. It's late and I'm tired.'

There's no *way he's security*. Jodie thought to herself.

'What are you really doing here?' she asked. 'I think we both know you aren't keeping an eye on the building.'

'Of course I am. Why else would I follow you down here?'

'Follow me down, you say?' Jodie replied. 'Before, you said you were just coming to check and you saw my car. Now you're changing your story?' She saw a flash of agitation cross his face. 'Just drop the lies, will you? Tell me what you want with the building.'

His jaw tensed, eyes flaring with anger. It was enough to make Jodie regret pushing back. *Why didn't you just go when you had the chance? Who gives a shit what he's doing here? Just go and leave him to it.*

The man suddenly advanced. It caused Jodie to jump in shock and she brought her hands up quickly, expecting him to grab her. Instead, he moved past her to the window she'd been creeping towards. There, he opened the latch and forcefully slid the window up before turning to her with a scowl.

'Get the fuck out. Now,' he seethed, all pretence gone.

'Calm down,' Jodie said, hands still raised. 'Stop being so—'

'Just get the fuck out!' he snarled. 'I haven't got time for this shit. Hop out the window, get in your car, and drive away. Now. I mean it.'

Jodie lowered her hands, scared but angry at how she was being spoken to. 'Or what?' she asked, immediately regretting it. *What the hell are you doing, Jodie? Don't antagonise him!*

He strode forward, coming close to Jodie and squaring up, his eyes burning into her. Jodie turned her head to the side and shrank down as she felt his warm breath on her cheek.

'I won't tell you again,' he said through gritted teeth. 'Leave now, or you'll regret it.'

Jodie again had a compunction to argue back, but this time thought better of it. It was obvious the man had no more right to be at Parson Hall than she did, but she knew it wasn't worth getting hurt over. Even so, backing down still didn't sit right. *But it's not like I have a choice.*

'Fine,' she reluctantly said. 'I'll go.'

His eyes studied her for a moment, then his body visibly relaxed. 'Good,' he said and stepped back, giving her space. She scowled back at him and moved towards the open window, still shaking with fear, anger, and adrenaline. 'Look,' he went on, his voice having lost its threatening tone, 'just come back tomorrow or something. Tonight, well, you really can't be here. It's honestly for your own good. Trust me.'

Jodie had no idea what to say to that. She wanted to ask more, but decided against it and started to climb out of the window. He offered his hand to help, but she ignored it, casting him one last death-glare as she stepped down onto the ground outside.

She backed away, keeping her eyes on him. 'Maybe I'll just call the police myself,' she said antagonistically once she was far enough away. 'Anonymous tip. Get them out here after I've gone. What would you think about that?' She knew she was needlessly lighting the touchpaper but just couldn't help it. It wasn't fair that he got to order her around just because he was bigger and scarier than she was.

The man moved closer to the window, placing one hand on the sill. He leaned out.

'I'm letting you go,' he said, his top lip curled in annoyance. 'If you want to make things worse for yourself, go right ahead. I have your licence plate. I can track you down from that, believe me. And I will. If you make things difficult tonight, then I'll come find you. I'm not a good person. I can make people suffer.'

'That supposed to scare me?' Jodie replied, still backing up while trying her best to keep her voice steady.

He grinned darkly. 'It already has, I can tell. Like I said before, go home. You want to come back tomorrow, be my guest. But for tonight, well… this place just isn't safe.'

Jodie frowned. 'What do you mean by that?'

He shook his head. 'It doesn't matter. I'm actually trying to help you. Now get out of here before I run out of patience.'

The man continued to stare at Jodie without blinking. She decided she'd pushed her luck with him enough and that it was best to leave while she could. While she had no idea if he'd truly carry through on his threat, it wasn't worth the risk. As Jodie took another step back, she remembered what had happened upstairs—the sounds and the opening door—and even considered telling the stranger that he might not be alone in the hall after all.

No, let that arsehole find out on his own, she thought.

Without saying anything more, Jodie turned and walked back to her car, feeling his eyes on her the whole way. Once inside her vehicle, she started the engine and flicked on her headlights, illuminating more of the building ahead. She saw the man was climbing out the window, and her initial response was to panic, thinking he'd changed his mind and was coming for her.

However, once out, he just stood and watched her, clearly waiting for her to go. She realised he was likely just going to go back to his own car after she left. She doubted he was leaving, but maybe he had to grab whatever gear he'd brought with him.

It took her a little while to turn her vehicle around, shunting backwards and forwards as she completed the rotation, but then she was on her way back down the track and away from Parson Hall.

She kept looking in her rear-view mirror and eventually lost sight of everything as both the man and hall were swallowed by the night.

With every meter she drove, anger built: at being pushed away from the hall, at being bullied, and at the unfairness of it all. The fact that she had been about to leave anyway before the man showed up was mostly forgotten.

She thought again about who he might be and what he wanted with the hall. After all, he'd said it himself: there was nothing worth stealing. So why did he need the place to himself? Then it hit her.

He was there for the same reason she was. He was looking for paranormal phenomena and he just wanted her out of the way. What other explanation was there? *The stuff about it being dangerous was obviously just a lie.*

As she approached the turn off to the main road, Jodie wrestled with the idea of going back—of telling the guy to go to hell, telling him he couldn't force her to leave. She then put on the handbrake and let the vehicle idle as she considered her next steps.

Go home. It's the right thing to do. Ignore what happened here.

She thought again of Tony, realising she'd actually had a lucky break there; if it had been a *real* security person, she'd be in deep shit right now. The reputation of *Spirit Hunters* would be in tatters.

But then Jodie thought of Mark. She remembered how she'd felt looking back down into the old hall from the balcony, reliving the proposal. She wanted that again; she wanted more time with her emotions there, to maybe help heal that festering wound that had lingered since his death.

And lastly, she wanted to know what the stranger was really doing there. The unanswered question felt like an itch she desperately wanted to scratch. Going back to confront him would be foolhardy, she knew… but maybe there was another way.

Jodie considered turning off onto the main road, moving down a little way to find a suitable place to pull her car over… then sneaking back to the hall on foot.

She shook her head again. *That's just as idiotic. Go home and stop being stubborn, Jodie. Stop being stupid.*

Jodie set the car in gear and pulled out onto the road, ready to go home and put everything behind her. After going no more than twenty feet, she saw a lay-by approach… which would be a perfect spot to leave the car.

No, stop it. Just go home. Be sensible.

Jodie drew closer and closer to the lay-by, trying to keep her focus on the road ahead. Then… she pulled the car in.

Jodie stopped the car and set the handbrake again.

You're a fool, she told herself. Fool or not, Jodie knew she was going back to Parson Hall.

7

THE WALK BACK DOWN THE DARK TRACK WAS EERIE, TO SAY THE least. Jodie kept to the side of the road and ensured the beam from her flashlight was aimed as low as she could make it. The last thing she wanted was to alert the stranger to her presence.

I'll just see what he's up to, she told herself, *then leave.* As she continued her isolated walk, constantly peeking into the tree line on either side of the road, she wondered again about the man. The idea he was from a rival ghost hunting company was still her best guess as to why he was there. He was alone, which was odd, but she guessed he could have just been a solo act—just like she was tonight. She knew most other companies and didn't recognise him from any social media channels, so there was a chance he was just starting up. If so, she resolved to make everyone aware of how he operated: threats and bullying.

But if you do that, Tony will find out you came out here.

Everything was quiet as Jodie walked, the only sound being her soft footfalls and the occasional chirping of insects in the trees and grass. It took a little over five minutes for the man's car to come into view again. Jodie pushed herself farther into the verge as she continued, eyes dead ahead, flashlight off.

Soon enough, she saw a moving light on the upper left-hand wing of the hall, indicating the stranger was inside. *I wonder if he will find anything waiting for him up there.* She hoped something *was* waiting that would absolutely scare the shit out of him to pay him back for the way he'd treated her.

Looking ahead, Jodie noticed the rear door of his SUV was open.

Still keeping her eyes on the upper floor, Jodie headed straight over to the vehicle and peered inside. The car was a mess, with rubbish and takeout wrappers strewn across both the front and back seats, and there was an almost overpowering stench of tobacco. But that was all cursory, and not what really drew Jodie's attention.

There were two large duffle bags on the back seat. On top of the bag nearest to her rested a thin manila folder, just sitting there, almost asking Jodie to take it and read it.

So she did.

There wasn't much inside, just a few sheets, but the first page looked to be a dossier on the building.

Strange.

She glanced back to make sure the man was still up on the top storey, then took the file and moved around to the back of the car, ducking down so she couldn't be seen. The action gave her another burst of adrenaline.

I feel like a spy.

She allowed herself a smile at the ridiculousness of it all, but she also realised a lot of the enjoyment came from defying the bully.

Jodie drew out her phone and illuminated the screen,

holding it close to the pages. The flashlight likely would have cast a glare, even if she was behind the car, but the phone was *just* bright enough.

Jodie began to read.

8

Dossier on Parson Hall

Built: Late 1682.

First owners: The hall was constructed and owned by the Holloway family. They were influential in the area, with deep ties to both the local church and many politicians. They were a contributor to the national Whig party.

Building uses: Initially, the hall was built for the community and lasted as a community hall until it left the possession of the Holloways. Over the years, the building expanded and was added to, becoming a stately home, orphanage, and even a boarding school for troubled boys. Eventually, it was reverted to a stately home once more when in possession of the Parson family.

. . .

Period(s) of note: 1890s.

Events of interest: Note—much of this information has been compiled from reports and statements following the events in the 1890s.

Nathaniel Barrow was employed at Parson Hall as an estate steward. Records indicate he was first employed in his late thirties. He was responsible for overseeing staff as well as the maintenance of the grounds. It is reported that Nathaniel was a quiet, reserved, and private man who didn't interact with others more than he needed to, usually hiding away in his designated working area in the attic space.

A year after Nathaniel was employed, stories started to circulate of him watching those under his stewardship. And not just watching them work, but spying on them. It seemed he had a penchant for voyeurism, though it was not purely sexual in nature, with Nathaniel coming to believe the building was his to protect, rather than him just being an employee there to fulfil a role.

It seems his obsessions grew over the second year, with reports of staff finding peepholes in the walls and ceilings. Years later, hidden passageways within the walls were also found, which Barrow had made to move around the property unseen. He'd been employed approximately two years when a young maid, Mary Dalton, was killed. At first, she had simply been considered missing, believed to have run away, but her body was found in the walls months later, and it was clear she had been strangled to death. The assumption was that she had stumbled across his hidden passageways and he'd been forced to protect his secrets. It isn't certain if the murder was premeditated, or if he'd simply panicked.

Documents were found in Nathaniel's quarters after his death: records of employees and their movements and schedules, including sleep patterns of those that stayed at the property, and also of how regularly they woke during the night. In addition, he noted how much each person could be 'trusted.' Over the years, those listed as untrustworthy went missing. In fact, so many people ended up disappearing that full investigations were launched, yet they came up empty. It wasn't until some renovation work was carried out in Nathaniel's sixth year that the head of a missing maid named Helen Gray was found, hidden beneath the floorboards in Nathaniel's room.

Word got back to the nearby village almost instantly. A mob of locals came up to the house and Nathaniel Barrow was brutally beaten to death, all before any authorities could be alerted. Stories state the enraged locals caught Barrow in the old hall and killed him there. It is unclear what happened to his body, with many reports saying he was buried on the property in an unmarked grave, left to rot and be forgotten.

Phenomena: While the hall was reported to be haunted long before the arrival of Nathaniel Barrow, happenings increased drastically following his death. Over the years, guests and people that lived at the hall reported much activity: feelings of being watched, the sound of footsteps, doors closing, heavy breathing coming from within the walls, even moving shadows and glimpses of a figure standing perfectly still in the corner of a room or by a window. Some guests told of hearing awful struggles and the sound of laboured breathing and gasping, as if someone were being strangled.

More interestingly, there were reports of physical contact, with people being woken up in the middle of the night, feeling hands around their neck. Two people felt themselves pushed just before falling down the stairs, and in

1954, a woman died after inexplicably tumbling down the flight of stairs close to the old hall.

Potential for a Dark Spirit: High.

The events surrounding Nathaniel Barrow drew a huge amount of dark energy to the location. In addition, he was killed at the property, so his spirit could well be tied there, as often happens in these situations. The plethora of activity in the years that followed—some violent—is all indicative of an active dark spirit.

Additional notes: Timing—the building has been on our radar for a number of years, but getting access during the stewardship of the previous owners proved impossible. A small window has opened now thanks to the prior owner's bankruptcy.

Anchor: We believe the anchor here is location based, being the building itself. As per normal procedure, the chosen Hunter will need to find the point of strongest energy flow to begin proceedings.

9

JODIE FROWNED IN CONFUSION BEFORE QUICKLY READING THE document a second time. *What the hell?*

Her mind was reeling at the outlandishness of what was written. The history of Parson Hall had been interesting, and had even helped fill in some blanks Jodie had about the place. But the stuff *after* that? Dark spirits, dark energy… Jodie had no idea what to make of it.

It didn't seem like the stranger had written the report himself, though. It referenced 'a hunter,' meaning the author of the report was not the person out in the field.

So the stranger upstairs is one of these... hunters? But a hunter of what?

All Jodie could think was that he was hunting the 'dark spirit' mentioned in the document. She wondered if it meant he was going to perform some kind of cleansing or exorcism. He didn't look like a priest, but that was all she could come up with. How else could one hunt a ghost?

Well, not a ghost. A dark spirit. Maybe it's different.

The whole thing seemed crazy to Jodie, and frustratingly, the report didn't give any clue as to its author: no name, no letterhead, no logos. Nothing, save for the text. The next sheets were printed floorplans as well as a map of the grounds, but again there were no titles or wording to indicate who had pulled them together.

After looking over everything that second time, Jodie pulled out her phone and took a photo of each page, using the flash, hoping it wasn't bright enough to stand out. Once satisfied she had what she needed, she also got a shot of the vehicle's licence plate. After all, the man had hers, so why not the other way around? *Two can play that game, bucko.*

Jodie set the file back inside the car and then stared at the two duffle bags. *Do I rifle through them as well?* She was about to, but the light inside the building appeared again, this time on the ground floor. Jodie's chest tightened as she realised the man might be returning to his vehicle.

After briefly considering her options, Jodie elected to run quietly *towards* the manor, hoping she could hide close to the wall and peek through one of the windows to watch what he was doing. If the man returned and exited the building, she could just stay on the opposite side to him. The window to the living quarters was still open, and she hoped the one to the old hall was as well. If it was, she could just use the window farthest away from the man when he emerged and get back inside, then hopefully spy on him to learn more.

She just had to make sure she stayed out of sight.

What are you doing? Just go home! You still can! The sane part of Jodie wasn't giving up, but her curious, rebellious side was still winning out. Barely.

As much as Jodie had found the man intimidating when he'd shown his anger, she didn't *really* believe he'd do anything to hurt her. After all, he'd let her go, so it was clear he didn't *want* to do anything, even though he'd had every opportunity to. He just needed the building to himself. Then, on top of that, once Jodie had agreed to leave, the man had actually extended an olive branch of sorts, saying she could just come back the next night when it was safe.

Her gut told her the stranger just didn't want her caught up in whatever was happening.

But you came back regardless, Jodie, she thought to herself. *So you're probably caught up in it anyway.* She jogged to the building, keeping her body low and footsteps light.

She headed towards the hall, which was quiet, then continued around the side of the building. As she did, she heard something that made her peek back again.

At the far end, she saw the stranger climbing out of the open window in the living quarters, the same window she'd exited from. His light bobbed while he made his way back to his car. She noticed that he was wearing a backpack now, and when he reached the vehicle, he pulled out one of the duffle bags closer to him, opened it, and began to rummage inside.

Jodie once again looked at the open window close to her.

Staying outside was safer if she didn't want to get caught, but if she intended to get to the bottom of everything, she'd need to see what he was doing for herself.

But is it worth it? Who cares what he's up to?

Though her internal struggle still wasn't resolved, she swung a leg over the open windowsill, giving in to her impulsiveness and recklessness.

That side of her nature had certainly been curbed after meeting Mark, and she'd kept a lid on it since his death, but tonight it was rearing its head again and making itself known. She'd built the night up to mean so much that she wasn't prepared to let it end early just because of a bully.

Plus, that dossier had piqued her interest. She wanted to know what was going on, what a dark spirit was, and what the stranger meant when he said things were going to get dangerous that night.

Once inside, Jodie paced over to the front of the hall, just to make sure the stranger was still over at his car, which he was. She then considered where she could go to hide.

Not just *hide. Spy.*

It was going to be difficult keeping out of sight, especially considering the lack of hiding places in each room. Plus, she had no clear idea of which room to go to first.

As she moved, Jodie used the screen from her phone rather than her flashlight application. The screen didn't cast much light at all, not even letting her make out the other side of the hall, but it was *just* enough to see where she was going.

She navigated to the closest stairs, thinking it would be easier to watch him from the first floor, and found the enclosed stairwell was even darker than the hall had been. Once on the stairs, she took a breath and looked up into the dark. Jodie was reminded of what she'd read in the dossier: of people being pushed down the stairs. Those were stories Jodie had already been aware of, but even so, they were now fresh in her mind. She placed her foot onto the first step, yet before she could continue, she heard a creak from higher up.

She whipped her head up in shock and aimed her phone higher, though the screen was too weak to reveal more than a couple of steps. Jodie waited, listening.

Creak.

Jodie's body locked up at the second noise, which sounded as if someone had descended another step. *Screw being stealthy.* She quickly pulled out her flashlight and clicked it on, aiming the beam up ahead, washing the stairwell in a piercing white spotlight that forced its way up to the half-landing. The stairwell was empty.

Jodie waited, body still tense, fully expecting another sound. Though she still hadn't seen anything, she couldn't shake the feeling that *something* was there. It felt like she was being watched by some unseen person, some unseen *thing,* on the stairs—invisible to the world, but present nonetheless. After a few moments, Jodie moved up another step before waiting again. Nothing came. She wondered if the creak had just been a natural groan from the house, caused by something mundane, like the movement of old materials.

Cautiously, she continued up, eventually stepping into the half-landing and turning around to look up the rest of the stairwell. She narrowed her eyes as she stared more intently, waiting for any kind of sound. She was about to move again when—

Thud.

A heavy footstep landed *directly* behind her, causing Jodie to jump. She spun, goosebumps springing up over her skin, noticing in that instant the sudden drop in temperature around her. Yet the flashlight showed only an empty space down the flight of stairs. Her hands shook and the light from her torch wobbled.

'Who's there?' she demanded, louder than she'd intended. Even as panic gripped her, part of her brain was telling her to calm down, but it was hard to listen.

The amount of activity in such a short space of time was disconcerting. That, coupled with seeing the boy at the Manor House only a few days ago… it just seemed like a *lot* was happening to her recently, almost like… something was building. Jodie dismissed the notion as crazy. *I'm putting myself in haunted locations. It shouldn't be a shock when things happen.*

She moved backwards, taking a step up onto the stairs but still looking down. Then, she ascended another step, then another, breath held, fully expecting to hear something else.

The noise that *did* come, however, was from farther away. While she couldn't be certain, Jodie's gut told her it was the stranger climbing back inside through the living quarters. She remained rooted to the spot, trying to figure out her next move, still anxious at the sounds she'd heard from the stairs.

I can't just hide away here all night. I'll get caught.

So, Jodie forced herself to keep taking slow steps backwards, rising up the stairwell, keeping the beam from her flashlight trained on the landing below.

Just as she was midway up the flight, Jodie felt another creeping sensation, like she was being watched again. She slowly turned, half expecting to feel a set of cold hands press on her and shove her from behind, again thinking about the stories of the people being pushed. Thankfully, the space above was clear, so Jodie quickly made her way to the top, keeping her footsteps as light as she could. While she moved, she briefly wondered if the activity she'd been experiencing since entering had somehow been triggered by the stranger's presence, but that didn't track—when the attic door had opened earlier, he hadn't arrived yet.

Maybe it's reacting to me, then. Just like at the Manor House.

Another thought then struck her, completely out of left field: *maybe the things here knew the stranger was coming.*

She quickly dismissed the idea, chastising herself for overthinking things. Jodie reaffirmed to herself that she was safe from the spirits there, as scary as they could be.

They can't hurt you.

But as she gazed down the stairs, again remembering the people that had been pushed, she knew that wasn't quite true. She thought again of what she'd experienced at her grandma's.

After then pulling herself back to the present, Jodie quickly moved out into the small corridor. Her eyes were immediately drawn to the door to the attic. It was still open. Looking at it caused another chill to run up her spine as she thought about what had happened up there with Mark and Tony.

10

Seven years ago...

'Well, it's lived up to the hype so far,' Mark said as the trio made their way along the mid-floor corridor. Jodie paced next to him, with Tony up ahead.

'Indeed,' Tony said over his shoulder, still facing forward. 'Cold spots, footsteps, even whispering.'

'Shame we didn't get evidence of it all,' Jodie added.

'True,' Tony said. 'But we've got *some*. And we'll get more, I just know it.'

Jodie cast her eyes to Mark, and the two shared a smile. Tony's enthusiasm was certainly infectious; it had been one of the driving forces in them setting up a company in the first place.

The corridor was well lit, with the group having turned on all lights so they could selectively turn off the ones they needed for seances or investigations.

'Shame the owners are selling it,' Mark said. 'Think we'll get to come back here before it changes hands?'

'Doubtful,' Tony said from ahead. 'I heard the sale is going through quickly, and the new owners have zero interest in things like this. Word is, they want people to forget the stories of the building being haunted entirely. So this is probably our one and only investigation here for the foreseeable future.'

The group continued on, heading towards the attic, which was on the top storey of the east wing. It was the primary area they had been keen to spend some time in, but they'd held off so far, focusing on the lower stories initially.

Saving the best till last.

Tony had two bags slung over his shoulder: a large rucksack and a camera bag housing a thermal imaging camera. Mark was carrying a host of audio equipment as well as the EVP recorder. That left Jodie with a duffle bag of her own containing the Ouija board—something they hadn't used yet —battery packs, and food and water supplies.

Once through the main corridor, the group traversed the connecting bedroom and the smaller hallway beyond, moving straight over to the stairwell that rose up. Their footfalls were heavy as they clomped up the stairs, soon emerging into an area at the top. There was no immediate door at the head of the stairs, the space instead opening out into a full-width vestibule area. The floor there was carpeted and the walls lined with plaster and decorated a plain white. The walls didn't run up far before meeting the pitch of the sloped ceiling with exposed thick oak beams. There was only a single light in the space, fitted to the middle of the pitched ceiling, though it was strong enough to illuminate the whole area. Straight ahead of the group was a short flight of four steps, and at the top, a door set into the cross wall. This gave access to the main attic beyond.

'You okay?' Jodie asked Tony, who was pulling in deep breaths. He was carrying the heaviest load—at his own insistence—despite being the oldest. He just waved away Jodie's worry, like he always did.

'I'm fine,' he said and started moving again, walking straight over to the door.

'It's okay to take a minute, Tony,' Mark said.

'Don't need a minute,' the other man replied.

Mark looked over to Jodie, grinned, and rolled his eyes.

'He won't listen,' Jodie whispered to him as the pair followed.

Tony opened the door and led everyone through to the main attic. It was decorated similarly to the vestibule area, but with bare floorboards, meaning their footsteps echoed through the long, triangular space. There were more lights than the vestibule, three this time, all fixed to the underside of where the chunky roof joists met. Jodie spotted two sloping roof windows, one on either side, though all that she could see through them was the darkness of night.

There was more furniture in the attic space, including four full-height, free standing mirrors with gold frames. Jodie knew they probably weren't *real* gold, but they still looked regal and impressive all the same.

There was also a tall set of drawers, some bench seating, waist-height circular tables, and a long, low chest.

'Huh,' Mark mumbled. 'For some reason, I just assumed this place would be full of junk. Like a storage space, you know? I expected it to be... creepier.'

'Looks pretty clean and orderly to me,' Jodie said as she gazed around. She moved to a mirror and looked at her reflection.

'So, what are we going to do first?' Tony asked. 'I can get the thermal camera going, just mount it on one of the tables and let it run. We can set the EVP equipment going as well.'

'We could try the board first,' Mark replied. 'Might as well get some use out of it, since we brought it.'

Tony nodded. 'Fair point.'

Jodie knew Tony wasn't overly enamoured with Ouija

boards, claiming they were easily manipulated. And while none of them would ever fake anything, any results from Ouija boards were generally looked upon with scepticism from the wider community. Regardless, Jodie still enjoyed those types of sessions. There was an undeniable thrill in thinking you might be speaking to someone that had crossed over.

With them all being in agreement, Jodie laid out the board on the floor while Tony set up some small electric lights and switched off the main ones. The portable electric lamps left them with just enough illumination to see each other and their immediate space, but little else. While Tony worked, Mark set up the thermal imaging camera, as well as an audio and video recorder.

The trio then sat cross-legged around the board, all leaning forward and placing the tips of their fingers on the planchette. Jodie made sure her touch was feather-light and checked to make sure there were no signs of pressure from any of the others as well. She trusted them completely, but she knew Mark wasn't beyond playing a practical joke every now and again.

'Who wants to start?' Tony asked.

Mark and Jodie looked at each other. 'I will,' Jodie said after a brief pause.

She took a breath and waited a moment. Everything was quiet, the absolute silence only broken by the electronic hum from the lights close by.

Before she could speak, Mark cut in, in his most theatrical voice: *'Is there anyone theeeere?'* Jodie snorted a laugh. Tony rolled his eyes, but was grinning as well.

'I saw that coming,' he said. 'You're too predictable, Mark.'

Mark shrugged. 'I like to think of it as being reliable.'

Jodie let things settle down for a second time, then took another breath. 'Is there anyone present that can hear me?'

she asked once she was ready. They waited, all looking at the planchette. 'Anyone at all?' she went on. 'Don't be scared. We want to listen.' Still nothing.

'Is Nathaniel Barrow here?' Mark asked. 'We'd very much like to speak with him. Nathaniel, can you hear me?'

The planchette didn't move.

Yet after a moment, Jodie heard the dull *click* of an opening door coming from downstairs. A slow *creak* followed.

The trio all lifted their eyes to each other. No one spoke, they just listened. Jodie held her breath.

Soon all was silent again.

'Can you give us another sign?' Mark pushed.

For the briefest moment, Jodie thought she felt a tremor in the planchette, but when she gazed down it was still stationary. After about ten seconds without anything else, she spoke again: 'How many people are here in the building with us? Is it just one?'

She kept her eyes on the board, hoping the slider would move to either *Yes* or *No*. It didn't budge.

Mark then asked: 'If someone *is* listening, can you tell me if you died here?'

All eyes stayed on the planchette. Jodie was about to follow up with a question of her own when the slider inched across the board. Her eyes widened and she again glanced to the others. Both of them appeared equally shocked as the planchette slowly scraped across towards the word *Yes*.

'Did any of you do that?' Tony asked, his eyes falling on Mark, suspicion obvious.

'I didn't, I swear,' Mark protested.

Jodie glanced down at the planchette again. 'I believe him,' she said. It didn't take much to move the slider on the polished surface, which was why Ouija boards were so inconsistent and often dismissed—sometimes people ended up moving the slider without realising—but Jodie knew Mark well enough to spot when he was lying or goofing around.

'Did... Nathaniel Barrow kill you?' Tony asked. The planchette started to slowly move away from the *Yes*, inching to the *No*. However, it abruptly stopped, then quickly slid back and settled onto the *Yes* once more.

Jodie felt a flood of excitement. 'Were you one of the maids?' she asked, eyes wide.

Yes.

'And was your body hidden in the walls?' Tony went on.

Yes.

'Is... is it still there?' Mark asked.

No.

'Were you buried?' Jodie followed up.

Yes.

Jodie hesitated, then asked: 'Can't you just move on?'

No.

'Why?' Jodie continued. The planchette wobbled, but didn't slide in either direction.

'We need to stick to yes-or-no questions,' Tony said. 'Easier for them to answer rather than spelling things out.'

Jodie nodded. *Considering the time period the girl lived in, she might not have even been able to read or write.*

'So, there's something keeping you here?' Tony asked, his narrowed eyes fixed on the board.

Yes.

A thought then struck Jodie. 'Is it... *him?*' she asked. 'Is Nathaniel somehow keeping you here?'

Another pause of the planchette, before it slid away, paused, then moved back to *Yes*.

She looked to the others, who cast frowns of confusion. 'Is he the one keeping the other spirits here as well?' Tony asked.

Yes.

Jodie turned her head to Mark. 'Can one spirit really anchor others to a location like this?'

Mark shrugged. 'I honestly have no idea.' His eyes moved questioningly over to Tony.

Tony thought about his answer for a moment. 'I don't know,' he said. 'I guess it's possible?'

'Are there many others here?' Mark asked the spirit. The planchette didn't move. Jodie watched the piece of wood intently, waiting for the answer. It remained completely still.

'Are you still there?' Tony asked. Still nothing. 'Can you hear us?'

'Please come back,' Jodie went on. 'Give us a sign.'

After a few more seconds, Tony let out a small sigh. 'She's gone.'

'Shame,' Mark said. 'That was some good stuff. Interesting that—'

The planchette moved, darting a few inches to the left—Jodie gasped.

'Are you back?' Tony asked.

The slider was once again motionless.

'Have you come back to talk to us?' Jodie pressed.

Finally, the planchette slid to *No.*

Jodie cocked her head. 'Are we still talking to the maid?'

No.

'Someone else, then?' Tony questioned, even though the answer was obvious.

Yes.

Mark leaned forward a little. 'Did you die on the grounds as well?'

A pause, then… *Yes.*

'Were you killed by Nathaniel?' Tony questioned.

Another pause. Jodie gasped as the electric lights around them flickered. The slider moved to *No.*

A creeping feeling worked its way over Jodie. 'Wait,' she whispered. '*Are* you Nathaniel?'

The lights flickered again; the planchette slowly moved to one side. She fully expected it to shift back to *Yes*. Instead, it suddenly shot out from their grasp and skidded off the board completely, drawing a gasp from Jodie.

The lights continued to flicker, flooding the space in a strobe-like effect. Jodie's hand quickly found Mark's and she squeezed, casting a frantic gaze around the room. The flashing made it hard to see anything, and she had to narrow her eyes to stop from being blinded. As she turned her head, her focus fell on one of the nearby mirrors facing them.

There, in the blinking lights, she saw their own reflections; every one of the trio looked panicked, all glancing behind themselves.

However, she saw something else as well.

In the reflection, there was a figure standing in the middle of them, positioned directly atop of the Ouija board. It was little more than a shadow, but with a clear human shape.

Jodie let out a cry of fright. Everyone turned to face each other, with Jodie's gaze quickly falling on the space above the board. The shadow was still there, looming over them.

'Jesus Christ,' Tony uttered, scurrying backwards. The shadow held its presence for a moment… then blinked away, becoming lost in the flashes of light.

Jodie pushed herself back, with Mark crawling quickly over to her.

Tony was moving quickly as well, and Jodie soon realised he was scampering to retrieve the planchette.

The Ouija board flipped itself over. Mark threw a protective arm around Jodie, whose heart was hammering rapidly in her chest. The lights continued to flash.

As scared as she was, Jodie was still in awe at what they

were experiencing. It was far beyond anything the group had seen since starting the whole ghost hunting venture.

But you've seen worse, she quickly reminded herself, remembering her youth.

'Turn the board over!' Tony commanded as he grabbed the planchette. Jodie moved forward and reset the board just as she heard the door to the attic slam shut.

The flickering of the lights sped up as Tony set the planchette. 'Everyone, get back into position.' He locked eyes with the pair and nodded.

Jodie knew what he intended to do, so she and Mark took their places again and everyone placed their fingers on the slider. Jodie tried to block out what was happening around her, focusing only on the board.

The trio themselves then moved the planchette across the board as it bounced beneath them. Finally, they settled the slider over the word *Goodbye*.

'Goodbye!' Tony called out, with Jodie and Mark repeating the word as well, which they hoped would close the connection.

In an instant, the flashing of the lights ceased, resuming their previous steady glow.

Breathing heavily, Jodie looked around the space, eyes searching the shadows, but there was an undeniable stillness in the area now.

They all waited, slowly trying to calm themselves down. It soon became clear that the activity was finished. Jodie let out a sigh of relief.

'Wow,' Tony said with a nervous laugh. 'That was... something.'

'You're telling me,' Mark added. He held out one of his hands, showing the others how it still shook. 'Scared me half to death.'

Jodie's body was trembling as well. Yet there was elation

mixed in with the fear. *That was the best encounter Spirit Hunters has ever had.*

After allowing themselves a few more moments to recover, Tony slowly stood up, stretching out his back. He walked over to the main switch and hit it, flooding the whole attic with more light. The man then moved around to the portable electric lights and flicked them off one by one.

'I just hope the recording equipment picked most of that up,' he said. 'The readings should be interesting.'

'Are we finished up here?' Jodie asked, getting to her feet as well.

'Not sure yet,' Tony said. 'Just thought we could do with more light until we make our minds up.'

Mark stood up beside Jodie, his eyes still looked wide, gazing at her with an expression she couldn't place.

'You okay, babe?' she asked.

He smiled and gave a firm nod. 'Yeah, actually. I am.'

Jodie cocked an eyebrow. 'Uh... okay.'

'We can do a few more sessions if we're all up for it,' Tony said. 'Or are we thinking that was enough for one night?'

'I'm happy to keep going,' Jodie replied enthusiastically. As scared as she'd been, the whole thing had just made her hungry for more.

The trio debated what to do next, and eventually settled on going down to the old hall again, since Tony was keen to spend more time in the oldest part of the building. After packing up the equipment, they made their way down. En route, Jodie noticed that Mark kept glancing over at her.

'What's gotten into you?' she asked him quietly with Tony a few paces ahead.

'What do you mean?' he replied.

'You keep... staring.'

He smiled. 'Just admiring your beauty.'

'No need for sarcasm,' she shot back with a grin.

But he took hold of her hand and squeezed it. 'I mean it,' he said.

She felt a sudden flutter of excitement at his words, even flushing a little. Normally, the couple playfully teased each other out of affection, so hearing him being so earnest was… different.

But entirely welcome.

Back down in the hall, Tony began setting up the recording equipment, ready for a seance. Just as Jodie stepped past Mark to go help, he stopped her, spinning her to face him.

'Seriously, what's gotten into you?' she asked. Her breath then caught in her throat as he slowly got down on one knee. 'What… what are you doing?' she asked in shock.

'I… don't know,' he replied with a nervous laugh. 'Well, no, I *do* know,' he went on. 'Jodie, this feels right. I didn't exactly plan it, so don't have a…' Mark shook his head and held her hand in both of his as he looked up at her. 'I'm not making sense, I know that. So…' Jodie saw him take a deep breath. 'Jodie, I've never been happier than I am with you. Being here tonight, it all feels… perfect. I want to keep doing this with you. I want to keep doing *everything* with you. Kids, a big house…' He grinned. 'Hunting more ghosts. I want it all.' Jodie didn't know what to say. She realised Tony was watching on in surprise. 'Jodie,' Mark continued. 'Will you marry me?'

The rush of emotion that swept over Jodie threatened to knock her off her feet—the sensation so intense she swayed unsteadily. In truth, she'd been thinking about marriage herself for the last couple of months but hadn't wanted to raise it for fear of scaring Mark off. She truly believed he was the best thing to happen to her: he grounded her, made her more responsible, but most of all, he made her happy.

'Yes!' she cried out and threw her arms around him.

'Absofuckinglutely *yes!*' She then smothered his cheeks in kisses.

'Bloody hell, Mark,' Tony said with a big smile on his face. 'How long have you been planning that?'

But Mark didn't answer. Instead he stood up, cupped Jodie's cheeks, and planted a long, firm kiss on her lips. Her heart raced.

Is this really happening?

It seemed so surreal. To be proposed to was a major life event, one Jodie hadn't been sure she would have ever experienced before meeting Mark—the idea of anchoring her life to another person had never sat well with her.

And despite the location of the proposal being slightly odd, it was actually all perfect. Mark spontaneously popping the question in a haunted house just... fit.

Mark gently rubbed her arms as they stood chest to chest, gazing into each other's eyes. He smiled, clearly ecstatic himself. 'Sorry I don't have a ring yet,' he said. 'Like I said, I didn't plan for this. Hope it didn't spoil the proposal.'

She shook her head. 'No, not at all. It was perfect.'

He kissed her once more. Jodie couldn't help but think about how their lives would change from that moment on. It didn't scare her, not one bit. It excited her.

It's perfect, she thought again.

11

Jodie's eyes remained fixed on the open attic door, wondering if she should go up. Memories of the experience with Mark and Tony swirled about in her mind. While it had all led to something good—something *amazing*—it had still been terrifying: the strobing lights, the flipped Ouija board, the shadowy figure—it had been *intense*.

But back then, at least she'd been in the presence of the others.

Now she was alone. Well… *almost* alone. There was the stranger, of course, but though Jodie's gut told her he wasn't dangerous, it wasn't like she trusted him.

In the end, Jodie decided not to venture farther up, because that would only block herself in. The attic had only one way in and out—unless she climbed out of the roof windows. *Plus hiding up there is gonna make it hard to spy on the guy.*

She paced over to the central corridor, and once there, switched off her flashlight and crept closer to the bank of windows. She peered outside.

All the doors on the SUV were closed, which only reinforced her belief that he'd already come back in. She listened intently, trying to pick up on movement... and a few minutes later heard it.

Again, Jodie asked herself why in the hell she'd come back. But instead of listening to that part of her mind, she focused on the little voice that told her to keep going and not be pushed around. She held her ground, trying to work out where the man was going. The movement continued across what she assumed was the corridor directly below her, then moved farther on.

He's heading to the old hall, she realised.

Jodie glanced back to the door to the interconnecting bedroom. Beyond that was the door to the mezzanine floor above the hall.

If I'm quiet enough, I can watch him.

It was risky, Jodie knew. She tried to remember if the mezzanine floor had been creaky when she'd walked along it earlier, but couldn't recall. If she moved slowly and steadily, Jodie hoped she could get right over to the handrails without drawing attention.

She also realised she wouldn't have a better opportunity to spy; it offered the perfect vantage point while still keeping her out of sight. So, Jodie crept quietly through the bedroom to the short hallway.

The door to the mezzanine was still ajar. *I'll just have to inch it open a little more. Hope the hinges don't squeak.*

Do it, she told herself. *And if he sees you, just be indignant.* After all, she didn't owe the man any explanations or apologies. Though she also didn't want to push things too far.

After moving forward, Jodie took hold of the door handle and gently pushed it. The door resisted at first, then moved, slowly gliding open. About halfway through opening it, Jodie stopped dead, feeling the hinges hit a small point of resistance. *If I push farther it'll creak.*

The man was in there. She could hear him shuffling around, though had no idea what he was doing.

Jodie looked at the door and realised it was open *just* enough for her to squeeze through. So, she turned her body sideways, sucked in her gut, and sidestepped through the narrow opening, shuffling carefully through the door. However, she froze when the handle snagged on her coat—the hinge squeaked. She held her breath and waited.

The noise had been very faint, but the rest of the building was fully quiet, so she had no idea if the sound had been loud enough to travel down to the man below.

She waited, realising his movements had stopped.

Shit.

Jodie listened intently, expecting to hear him head towards the door and then make his way up to investigate. Instead, he seemed to carry on with what he was doing; there came more sounds of shuffling and even something being unzipped.

After breathing a sigh of relief, Jodie unsnagged her coat and shuffled forward, eventually passing through the doorway completely. Once on the other side, she crouch-walked slowly out across the mezzanine floor. There came the glow from his flashlight below, and that light helped guide her way. She kept going until she was a few feet away from the guardrail. Once there, she lay face down and crawled the rest of the way, keeping her movements slow, steady, and silent. Eventually, she reached the edge and pushed her head forward to look down through the rails.

Thanks to the man's flashlight, which was set on the floor close to him, she had a clear view of what he was doing, though it didn't make any sense.

He had his duffle bags close by, all unzipped, with his backpack just next to him. The man knelt on a blanket that was laid out on the floor.

He was positioned to the left-hand side of the hall, and Jodie noticed there were multiple stones set in a large circle around the blanket. She narrowed her eyes to try to get a better look at those stones; they seemed circular with flat tops and were roughly palm sized. They weren't exactly uniform though, each slightly different shapes and sizes.

There were a number of other objects lying on the blanket with the man. The first thing Jodie noticed was a Victorian-looking hand lantern, which was currently unlit. The glass centre section was enclosed by black metal casing with a round rung-handle at the top.

The stranger held a bundle of white A4 papers and was intently studying the top sheet. He slowly set the papers down, then turned his attention to the lamp. Jodie watched as he unlatched the head and lifted off the top section of metal. He then pulled a lighter from his pocket and retrieved something from the blanket, which Jodie soon saw was a long, thin wooden stick, which looked quite similar to an incense reed. The man lit one end of the reed, and once it had caught flame, he lowered the reed into the lamp and held it there until the wick inside the lantern started to burn.

Jodie frowned in confusion as the man pulled his hand away, put out the stick, and replaced the lid on the lamp, unable to understand what she was actually seeing in the lantern.

What on earth?

The flame was burning a very light blue.

Jodie had never seen anything like that before. Not from a flame. If there had been a bulb inside it would have made sense, but from a natural flame? *I wonder if the wick has some kind of coating that causes the weird colour?*

The man then leaned over and switched off his flashlight, meaning the only light was now the flickering blue-white hue from the lamp casting its eerie glow around the space. The light didn't stretch as far as the beam had, since it wasn't as focused, but it did spill over a wider area.

Eventually, the man retrieved the papers and rose to his feet, picking up the lantern as well and holding it aloft. He coughed to clear his throat, then began to speak loudly, reading from the top page.

Jodie had no idea what language the stranger was speaking, but it wasn't English. It seemed the man himself wasn't fluent, as he kept tripping over his words and had to speak slowly. At a guess, Jodie thought it was East-Asian, but she had nothing further to go on than that.

Whatever the man *was* reading, it didn't take him long to get through, and once finished he paused for a moment before starting again. It was then Jodie realised she should be filming everything, just in case she needed the evidence.

She drew out her phone, set it to record, and zoomed the camera in on him. The image was grainy due to the light source being so far away, and Jodie had a feeling the sound would be muffled too, but hopefully it would be enough.

About halfway through the man's second reading, Jodie felt something. It was like an invisible pulse had washed over her, spreading out from the hall below and making her feel lightheaded. In that same instance, Jodie's phone just... blinked out.

She quickly tapped the screen but got no response. Confused, she then held down the power button for a few seconds, expecting the device to restart. Still nothing.

What the...?

Her attention was drawn back down below as the man slowly folded his papers and slipped them into his backpack.

He looked out into the hall around him and spoke again, this time in English.

'Come on, then... show yourself, you bastard. Let's get on with this.'

Jodie froze as the door creaked open behind her.

12

Joe Hurst glanced up as he heard the creak of a door up on the mezzanine above, just able to make out a figure duck away from the guard rails. He felt his body tense up.

Been in worse situations than this, Joe. Keep calm.

While that was true, the dangerous situations of his past were entirely human and natural—as natural as military conflict could be described as, anyway. But this was *very* different.

It's all for her, he told himself. *It'll be worth it if I get to see her again. Get to tell her... I'm sorry.*

He kept his gaze high, surprised at how quickly things had started to happen. The ritual of provocation had obviously worked, yet this was just the start. Full manifestation would take time. And whatever was up on the mezzanine might not actually be the thing he was there for. It could be one of the others.

Probably is, he realised.

Joe contemplated leaving the circle and wandering about the house. He didn't like being so... stationary. The runes of binding had served their purpose, and they weren't there to offer him protection, so there was no specific reason to linger in place. When he'd first been shown how to use them, he'd initially thought he would be safe inside them. If only he was so lucky.

The only true protection he had was some of the other tools he'd acquired. *Yeah... 'acquired.' Let's go with that.*

But even so, the tools didn't offer absolute protection, so he'd also have to rely on his wits to see the night through. And see it through he would. That was imperative. If Joe failed tonight, the thing left behind would become a true danger to the living.

There was no turning back. Everything was already in motion.

Failure also meant he would no doubt be joining the lost souls trapped at Parson Hall.

And that's something I really don't fucking want.

Joe had encountered many things in his life, experienced a host of traumatic events, but he'd never before seen anything that led him to believe the paranormal was real.

Not until recently.

Eventually he decided that being on the move was the right course of action, so he gathered up the items from the blanket and put them away. He wrapped the runes in cloth, then rolled them inside the blanket, before stuffing everything inside one of the duffle bags. The shard compass, echo glass, and—critically—the soul vessel, he kept with him, placing the glass and soul vessel into his backpack and keeping the compass in hand. *Shard compass and echo glass might come in handy again soon.*

While he didn't need the soul vessel straight away, it was *critical.* The most important weapon he had. Joe couldn't afford to lose that.

Once done, he put on the backpack and moved onward. He did have some recording equipment with him in the bags left behind, things that were more standard ghost hunting equipment, but he didn't really see a need to use them. After all, what could they show him that the spirit lantern and compass could not?

Joe was on high alert as he walked—constantly checking his surroundings, moving the lantern around in slow arcs, even looking behind himself at irregular intervals.

As he moved, he thought again of the woman he'd encountered in the building earlier. That had been a stroke of bad luck and had threatened to derail the whole night.

He'd been left with no option than to force her to leave. Time was of the essence. If he delayed, they might track him down, before he'd had a chance to prove his worth.

Even so, Joe felt bad for how he'd handled the whole thing with the girl. Dealing with 'civvis'—as he used to call civilians back in the military—had never been his forte, so after the woman had proven she wasn't going to be easily ushered away, he'd resorted to threats.

The shame still clung to him. In many ways the woman reminded him of his dear Gemma, in that she didn't seem the type to back down or be pushed around.

Still, what's done is done. The woman is gone. And in the end, being mean to someone was a drop in the ocean if it meant saving their life.

And saving their soul.

He left the hall and moved out into the entrance corridor, where he gazed around intently, almost willing something to happen. He *hated* the waiting, the anticipation. He looked down and studied the shard compass in his hand.

It was the size of a pocket watch, with brass casing and a cracked glass covering. In many respects it looked like a normal compass, except the needle itself was a dark, jagged shard of... well, Joe didn't know exactly what. The shard spun slowly around, often changing its direction, indicating energy on all sides.

That was to be expected.

When he'd first arrived, the compass had been useful for honing in on the right spot to start the ritual. The place where the dark energy was strongest. Now, it would serve as an early warning system for any presence that might approach. At the moment the shard was still dull, devoid of a glow, which meant there wasn't anything in his immediate vicinity.

A sudden noise from upstairs caused his head to snap up.

It sounded like footsteps—someone moving quickly out from the mezzanine floor. Joe weighed up his next move. Did he go and confront whatever was up there, or just let things progress and simply continue ahead?

While keeping out of the way had its appeal, he knew that didn't make him safe. *Nowhere* in the building was safe now. Plus, part of him wanted to see the kind of thing he would be dealing with, just to break the ice. This was his first mission, hopefully the first of many, and he needed to make sure it was a success. Therefore, he needed to get used to facing off against the things summoned by the ritual.

And Joe *had* to keep doing this. The answers he needed depended on it.

I have to prove them wrong.

Even so, he was also wise enough to realise rushing into dangerous situations was usually ill advised. And with that in mind, he decided to continue along the ground floor to see what he could find there. After all, there was nothing he could *really* do until the dark spirit had fully manifested.

Nothing but survive.

13

After hearing the door creak open behind her, Jodie ducked away from the handrail to make sure she was out of sight and stared ahead at the now fully open door, though she saw only blackness beyond. The blue light below shone a little brighter, and she knew the man must have raised it higher after hearing the creak.

She felt a tingle of anticipation. The blue light from below didn't stretch far enough for her to be able to see much beyond the door—indeed, she could barely even see the door itself. And using her own flashlight was out of the question.

Jodie eventually pocketed her phone again—now seemingly useless—and inched forward a little, hoping to be able to see through more of the shadows, but it proved pointless. The darkness was simply too thick.

The light down in the main hall started to sway and was accompanied by soft, echoey footsteps. Jodie didn't know what to do. The open door ahead certainly didn't look inviting, yet there was nowhere else to go. And the stranger downstairs was likely on his way up to investigate. If Jodie stayed where she was, she would be found.

So, she decided to head into the dark. She'd been in haunted buildings before, experienced phenomena, and an opening door was nothing new to her. In times past, she would have approached the door with glee to investigate further, pushing past her trepidation. She needed that same resolve now.

After steeling herself, Jodie pressed forward, keeping low and making sure she was as silent as possible. She had to fight the temptation to flick on her flashlight as it soon became difficult to see, but eventually made it into the corridor. Once she was a few steps in, she then felt comfortable flicking on her torch; she'd heard the man exit the hall beneath and knew her light-spill wouldn't reach him. Once in the hallway, she aimed her beam over to the open door to the attic, just to make sure nothing was there. She then headed to the interconnecting bedroom. That way, if the man came up the flight of stairs close to her, as she suspected he was going to, she wouldn't be nearby.

Jodie also decided it was maybe high time she left Parson Hall altogether. She had him on video—doing God knows what—but with her phone now dead, what more could she really get? She just hoped there was a way of reviving the device and recovering the video, otherwise her coming back would have been pointless.

It's already pointless, she told herself. *You came back here out of stubbornness and nothing else*. While she knew that was true, the only other thing she could gain from staying was to confront him, yet watching him in the hall had unnerved her, so doing that was unlikely.

She couldn't shake the feeling he had been performing some kind of ritual.

After taking a few steps towards the bedroom, Jodie heard another hinge creak. She slowly turned towards the attic door and saw that it was now a little farther open.

Something wants me to go up there, she realised. The door opening was an invitation. But Jodie shook her head. *No chance.*

She repressed a shudder and took another step away from the doorway, facing forward once more. However, after no more than two steps, a sharp inhalation behind her caused Jodie to whip her head around again. The beam from her flashlight fell on the open door—Jodie immediately clamped her hand over her mouth to keep from screaming.

There was someone on the stairs.

The person was standing on one of the higher steps, meaning their upper body was cut off from view through the doorway, so Jodie could only see a pair of bare legs and feet, as well as the hem of a dirty old dress. The woman's dull-grey flesh had patches of decayed green. Her toenails were black, and some of the skin around the person's shins and ankles was peeling off. The legs were perfectly still, not even showing a natural sway.

Jesus Christ!

Jodie quickly took a step back, then turned and ran. Seeing a ghost fully formed like that was… well, it just didn't happen often. Almost never, in her experience.

Hell, even the child she'd seen at the Manor House had only been captured on video for a few frames. It hadn't actually been visible in the flesh. But this…

This was like her experience at her grandma's. And that meant danger.

Jodie bolted through the connecting bedroom and out into the corridor, stopping halfway down to turn back around and aim her light again, just to make sure nothing was following. Her breathing was quick and frantic.

There was nothing behind her. Even so, Jodie now knew without question it was time to go. Too much was happening, too much she couldn't control. *This whole trip has been a mistake.*

She felt a pang of guilt toward Mark, as if she were failing him by leaving, but she knew she had to ignore that. Things had gone too far.

She would let the stranger have the hall all to himself. *Let him deal with whatever is happening.*

So, Jodie continued down the hall, heart still racing and doing everything she could to keep the building fear at bay. She finally moved through the door at the end, into the hall and landing area at the top of the stairwell. Her body locked the second she heard movement below, the sound of footsteps coming closer.

The stranger.

She instinctively switched her flashlight off and waited. Soon, she saw a faint blue glow from the lantern wash up the stairs.

She silently cursed herself, having been sure the man was going to use the stairs on the other wing.

Damn it.

If he *did* start to come up, that meant Jodie would have to retrace her steps—back towards the apparition. She paused, holding her breath, waiting to see if the man ascended.

Jodie heard him slowly moving around, and then the light dimmed to nothing; she realised he'd entered one of the rooms down below.

Is he just... looking around?

It didn't make sense to Jodie. She knew he'd heard the creaking door to the mezzanine, and he *had* to have heard her running, so... why wasn't he coming to check? It would have been one thing if the noise had scared him and he'd bolted, but he seemed to be just casually wandering the building.

Which, she soon realised, meant he'd probably *expected*

something to happen. It was the only explanation she could think of. And that gave more credence to her notion that he had been performing some kind of ritual back in the hall.

That, plus the blue lantern, the circle of stones, and the weird things she'd read in the dossier, made it obvious he was caught up in something Jodie *really* didn't want to be a part of.

With the man still directly below her, and seemingly in no rush, Jodie knew she was going to have to go back the way she'd come. As scary a thought as it was, heading that way would at least bring her down closer to the hall. From there, she could dash out of the window and run, just sprint down the long road and back to her car.

It wasn't much of a plan, but it was something.

Though it took sheer willpower to move, Jodie headed back down the main corridor once more, flashlight on, keeping her eyes up ahead, breath held. The whole time, she saw those decomposing legs in her mind's eye.

As she walked, she wondered if the better option was just to go down, confront the man again, and then hope he let her leave.

As she reached the bank of windows, she allowed herself a brief pause to look outside. How she longed to be out there, away from the confines of the building; she'd take feeling exposed in the open air to the claustrophobic terror she was currently experiencing in a heartbeat.

Jodie set off, still not hearing the man ascend from below. After once again entering the interconnecting bedroom, she slowly crept towards the door that would access the short hallway beyond. Just as she placed her foot down on one particular spot…

Creak.

Jodie paused and looked down in confusion. The creak hadn't actually come from her—it had come from *behind* her.

She slowly turned, aiming the light back at the door she'd just entered through, just in time to see a shadowy figure duck back out of sight. In the instant it had pulled back, Jodie was sure she had seen glinting eyes reflecting in her light.

She tensed up again. *Shit, shit, shit.*

Jodie backed up. The amount of activity she was seeing in Parson Hall was staggering. There had been *some* after she'd first arrived, but ever since the stranger had entered things seemed to have jumped into overdrive. It wasn't normal. Even for the *para*normal.

She kept the beam from her flashlight trained on the door, focusing on the side where she'd seen the figure.

'Is… is someone out there?' she whispered, her voice cracking. 'Do you have a message for me?'

Jodie waited for some kind of response. When none came, she had another idea. A stupid one. Instead of running, she decided to see what she was dealing with. Jodie inched forward, slowly moving towards the door. Once there, she angled herself and leaned forward, flashlight held out, so that she could see the hidden space beside the doorway.

No one was there.

While Jodie knew that didn't mean the spirit was gone, she still felt a small amount of relief at everything being clear. She gritted her teeth together and moved back through the bedroom once more, not stopping until she was out in the short corridor.

She glanced at the door to the attic, remembering the legs, then quickly made a beeline for the staircase. She took the door to the landing while shining her light down the stairs.

Her eyes were growing strained from having to constantly use her flashlight, always focusing in on a narrow spotlight while everything around it remained hidden in shadow. She couldn't help but lament the fact the electricity was cut off, as a fully lit building would make her escape much easier and less panic inducing.

The staircase below her, drenched in black, felt just as ominous as when she'd first ascended, when she was certain she'd felt the presence of something. Stories of people being pushed again swirled in her mind.

Just go! Jodie ordered herself, knowing she couldn't afford to let her mind wander to places like that. It just kept her rooted to the spot in fear.

Before placing her foot on the first tread, she listened out, cocking her head to the side, trying to make out where the man was, hoping she could hear him. However, she couldn't hear anything, which meant he had to be in a different wing. *Or he's close by but sneaking around.*

Regardless, it was time to go. Jodie took the first step and began her descent. When she was midway down to the half-landing, she decided to look over the handrail, down to the next flight, just to make sure the coast was clear.

It was not.

A woman was crouched on the stairs, looking back up at Jodie, eyes wide and skin mottled. She was wearing what looked like an old maid's uniform, dusty and torn, and her greasy black hair was up in a loose bun. There were dark veins under her yellowy-grey skin, and the dark pupils of her eyes were abnormally large. The woman's jaw hung open, her face expressionless.

Jodie gasped in horror. She wanted to cry out, but her voice was trapped in her throat. She watched as the woman's expression changed; a sinister grin slowly spread over her lips.

Then the ghostly woman suddenly lunged, scuttling forward at frightening speed. Jodie found her voice and screamed in terror.

14

JOE COULDN'T HELP BUT JOLT AT THE SUDDEN SCREAM FROM across the building. It was then followed by what sounded like someone running up some stairs and a door slamming.

Keep calm, you know what this is.

He'd always prided himself on handling his nerves exceptionally well, and that trait had been useful in firefights, but something about his current situation made things difficult for him.

It was the unknown, he realised. With a person, you could talk to them, reason with them, even put a bullet in them if needed. He knew where he stood with that.

But this…

He didn't know the rules. Didn't know if there *were* any rules.

And that scream...

For some reason, he'd truly thought it had come from a living person, not a spirit. But he knew that wasn't possible. It had to be the things here, the ones being drawn into reality, instead of straddling the living world like they had been.

It is all part of the process. He'd been briefed about all of this when initially trained and knew what to expect. Well, *kind* of knew.

Even so, there was still that nagging feeling in his gut; the scream had sounded all too real.

Ignoring it for now, he headed out of the dining room and decided to check out the sitting room next door, guided by the lantern's eerie light. He wished he could've just waited outside the building while things happened, but that was expressly forbidden. For one, part of a hunter's role was making sure no members of the public happened to enter a location while the manifestation was in progress. But more importantly, a hunter was *part* of the ritual. The dark energy needed a living presence to latch on to and feed off of, to anchor itself to. Simply starting the ritual and running away would just increase the energy surrounding a location, but it would be unfocused and even more chaotic, leading to a major problem going forward.

As he entered the sitting room, he thought again about the possibility of death. He knew there was a very real risk. After all, he was a replacement for a previous hunter that had died, a man named Eli. Eli had also been in the military, S.A.S, which was a step above what Joe himself had been.

Probably why he was fully accepted.

The idea that a former member of the S.A.S had met an early demise in this line of work was concerning, though Joe knew Eli's own mistake had led to his downfall. He didn't know the details surrounding that mistake exactly, but it was still food for thought.

I just have to succeed. Then those with answers will take me seriously and let me continue.

Then, he could see Gemma once more.

Almost as soon as Joe entered the sitting room, the compass began to hone in on one specific direction. He saw the first signs of a blue hue start to take hold in the shard.

There wasn't much to see in the study, same as in the other rooms; the whole building had practically been gutted. As Joe followed the needle to the side wall, a light knocking came from it. He stopped and listened.

Tap, tap, tap.

The sound was coming from the corner of the room closest to him, as if someone was on the other side, in the dining room. The shard's glow was growing stronger.

Joe thought to the words he'd been told when first training, back before those in charge had changed their minds.

'They'll try to mess with you. Scare you. They'll feed on your fear before they try to hurt you.'

This was the start, he realised. The scream from upstairs, the knocking—a first attempt at trying to scare him and feed off him.

He took a step closer to the wall, raising his lantern. If the entity was on the other side, the lamp was obviously not going to show anything, but he lifted it anyway, instinctually more than anything else. Lantern aloft, he let its glow wash over more of the wall.

Tap, tap, tap.

Joe frowned. At first he'd assumed the sound was coming from the other side, but now… it was almost as if the knocking was emanating from *within* the wall itself.

He took yet another step closer, remembering the information from the dossier about how Nathaniel Barrow's victims had been hidden inside the walls. Hell, the man himself had fashioned secret passageways within some of them.

Maybe this was him. The Watcher of Parson Hall.

Tap, tap, tap.

Joe stepped right up to the wall and examined it. He didn't move his head *too* close to it, of course—he wasn't about to risk pressing his ear up against the plaster and let a hand come shooting out to grab him.

Bang, bang, bang.

Joe sprang back. The plaster wobbled and cracked at the blows that came from within. Just like he'd thought, it was as if someone was pounding on the inside of the wall.

Bang, bang, bang.

Joe stared wide-eyed, lantern still aloft, forcing himself to remain calm, fully expecting the sounds to continue… but they didn't. He waited… ten seconds, twenty, half a minute, yet the striking didn't return.

'Who's in there?' he demanded, remembering more of his brief training. *'You can communicate with them... if they're willing to talk.'* Joe again waited, listening for some kind of response, *any* kind of response. After he was met with more prolonged silence, he pocketed the compass, then raised his own fist and rapped his fingers on the wall.

'Hello? Anyone in there?'

The knocking returned: *Tap, tap, tap*. It was then followed by a pained, husky female voice, muffled by the wall.

'Come... in here... with me.'

Joe stepped back. *Not on your life*. 'So you *are* still here? How about you show yourself?'

'I... will. In... here...'

The whispered, cracked voice was almost taunting. Joe had no doubt it was the spirit of one of Barrow's victims, but that didn't matter. Given the dark entity's influence, he planned to consider all ghosts in the location hostile. They had no agency of their own, mere puppets of the darkness that had grown there, festering over the years.

'Come... inside...'

Though strained, it was as if the voice was trying to be alluring, almost seductive. Joe knocked on the wall again.

Not to draw a reaction, but to help determine what the wall was made of.

The sound of his rapping indicated the wall was not solid, and as he tapped a few other places, he guessed it was a timber-stud construction.

Wouldn't take much to break through, he knew.

Joe hesitated, trying to determine what he'd achieve by smashing a hole in the wall, and also attempted to figure out just why the idea was appealing to him. All he could think was that it would reveal the ghost. Then he'd finally see one of the things he was dealing with. Maybe that was enough of a reason.

Because so far, all he'd experienced was noises. He wanted to know his enemy. To see it. If he knew what the entities looked like, it wouldn't be a shock farther down the line.

Joe considered it a little longer. He knew he wouldn't feel good about kicking in the wall of an old property like this. He wasn't a vandal, but then again, the building wasn't exactly in the best condition anyway.

And he'd done much worse. He'd been involved in skirmishes that had obliterated entire buildings.

So what's one little hole?

He waited for a moment more, just to see if the spirit inside offered anything else, then he set the lantern down on the floor, straightened up, and set himself. Joe raised his foot and drove it forward with a grunt. Given his background in martial arts, he was flexible enough to strike the wall a little below his head height, and his foot went through on the first try, sending a shower of debris drifting down to the ground. The hole left behind wasn't big, but he was able to pull away more plaster with his hands, creating an opening around a foot wide.

Let's have a look at you, he thought, and retrieved the

lantern once more, which he raised up, illuminating the wall and the hole. Inside, he could see old timber studwork as he'd expected, with two frames visible: an inner frame and an outer frame with a gap of around a foot between them. Big enough for someone to hide in.

Hide and watch people.

However, there was no spirit as far as Joe could see, so he slowly leaned forward to investigate more.

The shadows in the wall were pushed farther and farther back by his light when he peered inside and to his left.

He stopped—a woman was inside. Joe almost gasped as he saw her, crouching down but looking up at him, eyes glinting white under the glow from the lantern. She wore a snarl on a face that was heavily decomposed, with areas of skin completely rotted away and showing only bone beneath. She turned her head, moving it away from the light, wincing.

Joe pulled back a little, instinctively moving away from the sight. He'd seen some awful things in his time, but this…

The sheer impossibility of it was almost too much to comprehend. The fear that seized his chest wasn't one he'd known before, brought on by something he could only describe as… otherworldly.

Though he'd inched back a little, he could still see the woman gazing up wildly through the hole, holding up a hand to protect itself from the light. It was then he noticed a bone jutting out of her neck at an awkward angle.

Okay, so I've seen one. Now what? he thought.

He had eyes on the spirit, but… there wasn't really much he could do. The soul vessel wasn't for her. So, he watched and waited. Soon, the woman pulled back with a strained snarl, moving deeper into the wall and out of sight. Joe leaned forward again in response, the hairs on the back of his neck still standing on end.

Eventually, she'd shifted back so far the light no longer reached her. And with her now hidden, Joe was forced to slowly push his head fully into the hole to try to see more. The woman remained out of sight. He quickly reached into his pocket and checked the compass again, only to see the shard now devoid of its glow and slowly rotating, unable to get a clear focus.

She's gone, he realised. *Pulled back through the veil.*

Still, he figured the fact she had been hiding in the wall might be a clue as to her death. Perhaps it was the place she'd been stored by Barrow after being killed. He wondered if he was in the room she'd actually died in.

Worth checking the echo glass, he thought.

So, Joe slipped off his backpack and drew out the glass. It was a small, oval, handheld mirror, with the glass face being about six inches in height. The mirror had an antique silver frame with a handle to the bottom, and the back had symbols carved in it that Joe didn't fully understand.

The glass face itself looked darker than that of a normal mirror, as if it had some kind of film across its surface, though Joe knew that wasn't the case. It was what was *behind* the mirror, lined between the glass and the metal casing, that gave it the darkened effect.

He remembered what he'd been told about the echo glass:

Mirrors are a window, and this is a window to the past. Though you might not wish to see what it shows.

At the moment, Joe *did* want to see. He felt like he *should* see. After all, if he was to continue in his role as a hunter, he had to get used to the toys a hunter used.

Joe held up the mirror and angled it so the reflection gave him a view over his shoulder, and he turned his body so he was facing the wall. Then he slowly rotated, sweeping across the room.

Eventually, he stopped, narrowing his eyes, trying to determine if he was seeing something. He held his position, and a moment later his suspicions were confirmed.

There was movement in the reflection, extremely slight, and barely noticeable. It was like he was seeing a shadow, only instead of the shape being dark it had a white hue, juxtaposing against the darker background. The shadow had a human form, which became clearer as the seconds passed. Joe tracked the figure through the reflection as it started to walk.

Moving with purpose.

Then, as the shadow came close to the wall, Joe noticed a second white shadow on the ground, arm held up in supplication.

Bingo, Joe thought.

The standing shadow—which he guessed was Barrow—started gesturing wildly with flailing arms. The figure on the ground shuffled backwards, hand still aloft, cowering in fear.

Joe allowed himself a brief glance back over his shoulder, away from the mirror; the actual space there was empty, indicating the reflection was indeed replaying events from the distant past. He turned back to the mirror and continued to watch.

The longer he did, the clearer the blurry white shadows became. He had been told if he watched long enough, more details would come through, and the shadows would even turn into full reflections of people. But he'd also been told that the longer he replayed the events in the echo glass, the more the dark energy would be drawn to it, the glass acting both as a window to the past and a beacon to the darkness in the present.

Initially, Joe had been confused as to why that mattered, and had asked, *'After the ritual, won't I be the anchor? The darkness will be drawn to me regardless.'*

The other man had agreed, but replied that the glass acted as an extra pull, bringing entities to him that might not be wanted.

Given it was Joe's first mission, he didn't exactly feel like increasing the focus on himself, yet he couldn't help but watch a little longer. He saw Barrow lean down over the fallen woman and grab her around the neck.

The woman's head lolled back and forth as Barrow shook her. She looked to be fighting against him, hitting back, but Barrow only leaned in, clearly applying more pressure. Joe watched as the woman's movements began to slow. The two white shadows began to sharpen even more, their fuzzy edges crystallising. Eventually the woman stopped moving, but Barrow held his grip.

That was Joe's cue and he lowered the mirror, having seen enough.

He'd seen death, plenty of it. But it was the avoidable death, the death of innocents, that always stuck with him and revisited him in his nightmares: civilians caught up in a hail of gunfire, or trapped in a building that was hit by artillery.

It had always gnawed at him.

Joe had no doubt the woman he'd just seen murdered had done nothing wrong—after all, what could *possibly* have justified that killing? She'd lost her life simply because Nathaniel Barrow had decided that was what had to happen.

Joe felt a sudden swell of hate towards Barrow, even though the man had been dead for over a hundred years.

However, his hate was suddenly tempered as a voice sprang up.

You're no saint, he was forced to remind himself. *Innocents have died because of you too, Joe.*

He remembered the child and his hate swiftly turned inwards.

Joe placed the mirror back into his pocket, then took a

breath, wanting the Ritual of Provocation that he'd started to hurry up and complete so he could push on. He wanted to shout at the empty space, to goad the spirits, in order to prompt some kind of response, some kind of action, but refrained. That was only his own frustrations coming out, his own self-loathing bubbling up to the forefront. Giving in to that would have been reckless.

And he'd learned from horrible experience that being reckless *never* amounted to anything good.

Maybe you can do some *good here,* Joe told himself. It was a thought he'd had prior to arriving, though it wasn't his main driver for coming. Still, he figured that if he finished what he'd set out to do, the ghosts currently caught in the black hole of the dark spirit—puppets forced into a hellish existence—would be released.

And that was... something. It wouldn't heal him of the grief he carried, but maybe it would sooth it, like a cooling salve on a burn wound.

Joe walked out from the room, trying to decide where to go next. He knew he was wandering aimlessly, waiting, but there was nothing else to do. In truth, he'd expected things to have been a little more... frantic... after completing the ritual. After all, he was the only living thing in the building, the only person there for the darkness to focus on.

For a horrible moment, he suddenly questioned if there really was a dark spirit there at all—maybe the maid he'd just seen was merely part of a normal haunting.

But he soon dismissed the notion. He'd searched the house with the shard compass and echo glass and had seen evidence. The shard compass had glowed just as it should have and guided him to the right spot; he'd also felt the pulse after successfully provoking the dark spirit.

No, he knew there was no mistake. There *was* a dark entity present. Joe just had to be patient.

Another scream from the level above sharpened his focus. He paused, then took a breath.

I guess it's time to go upstairs.

15

Jodie had sprinted back up the stairs and out into the small hallway, the crawling woman pursuing her. The spirit had moved like a spider, scampering entirely too fast. Jodie had *just* managed to slam the door shut as the groaning spectre had leapt forward.

Staring at the shut door, Jodie backed away, keeping the shaking light from her torch trained directly on the door, body locked in fright and eyes wide. She fully expected the door to be flung open and that awful thing to come scuttling out.

But Jodie was met with silence. There hadn't even been a *thud* of the entity colliding with the door. Just… nothing.

The silence felt heavy, wrong—as if the building was simply holding its breath, waiting for the right time to roar.

With no intention of going to the attic—the door to which still hung open—Jodie backed away to the connecting bedroom again, knowing the only other way she could head now was back across the corridor to the far wing.

The idea of the stranger finding her didn't worry her anymore. In fact, the thought was appealing. Having company in a place like this, even angry company, was better than being alone. *Safer* than being alone.

For the first time, Jodie decided it would be a good idea to actually seek the man out.

She continued to back up, then turned and opened the door to the bedroom, forcing it back just a crack…

…but then stopped. In the narrow gap, Jodie saw a face staring back out at her.

She gasped and jumped backwards, quickly yanked the door shut again, and scrambled away.

The face had been that of a male, and his skin was grey with patches of purples. There had been an awful indentation on the left side of his head, just above a ruined eye that hung from its socket.

As she was still processing what she'd seen, a slow, deliberate knocking came from the other side of the door.

Tap, tap. Tap, tap. She heard a gravelly chuckle, then more knocking. *Tap, tap. Tap, tap.*

Jodie felt a sudden urge to cry. The fear was getting to be too much. Far beyond anything she'd experienced during her previous investigations. In fact, she had only felt fear like this one time before in her life.

Just like then, she was in danger now. The amount of full-bodied apparitions wasn't normal, even in the world of ghost hunting. Something was very wrong with Parson Hall. She knew that now without question.

Though it took a monumental effort, she was able to summon her legs into action, turning and moving away from the door, but soon stopped short again, realising she was out of choices.

She had nowhere to go.

The only option was up into the attic, but Jodie wasn't about to do that. Which meant she had to stay where she was.

Shit!

Jodie looked again to the door where she'd seen the crawling maid and wondered if the woman was still in the stairwell. The teasing raps on the bedroom door behind continued. *Tap, tap. Tap, tap.*

'Shit!' Jodie seethed, aloud this time. She didn't know what to do. It wasn't even like there were any windows in the hallway, just two doors that led to exits, and both were blocked off. Though there was also the door to the attic.

The attic has roof windows, Jodie quickly said to herself. But she dismissed the idea. Climbing across a roof just wasn't going to happen.

Tap, tap. Tap, tap.

Jodie trembled with fear, though she knew she couldn't just stay rooted to the spot. Her eyes again fell on the door to the stairwell, and she wondered again if the maid had left. As much as it terrified her to do so, she knew she needed to check. Better that than just waiting for something else to happen.

So, after taking a steadying breath, Jodie aimed her light at the door and slowly started to walk forward.

Please be gone, please be gone, please be gone.

She tried to convince herself that because something was now in the bedroom behind her, the maid had to have vanished. She had no basis in reality for that to be the case, simply hope.

On the other hand, it did seem to be quiet beyond the door, so she kept her eyes forward, ignoring the continuing *tap, tap* from the other direction. Yet just as she was a few feet from the door to the stairwell, the tapping stopped.

Jodie halted. A frown crept over her face. She slowly turned her head just in time to see the bedroom door start to drift open.

Creeeeak.

The man with the dangling eye stood in the doorway, illuminated by her flashlight: his head was tilted to the side, mouth slack and jaw hanging open. He wore dusty, dark blue overalls and his dark hair was greasy and slicked down to his scalp.

Jodie felt a scream building, ready to burst free. But before she could let it, the door to the stairwell was flung open as well, slamming into the sidewall. The decomposing maid came stumbling forward like a zombie, arms outstretched and mouth open wide, her black tongue snaking down to her chin.

Jodie's scream finally burst free. 'Stay away from me!' she cried, frantic. 'Keep away!'

She instinctively ran, utterly terrified, and sprinted the only way she could: up to the attic.

Once in the narrow stairwell, Jodie slammed the door closed behind her. She then sprinted upwards, her feet thundering on the steps. The beam from her flashlight shook wildly as it guided her, revealing peeling wallpaper on either side and the bare timber treads of the stairs, which only served to amplify her footfalls.

She raced up to the vestibule area, where the floors were no longer carpeted as she remembered, now exposed floorboards. Loud banging came from the door behind her, as if two sets of hands were slamming against it.

Jodie kept her focus on the door ahead that led to the main attic space—an area her instincts were screaming at her not to go.

The sloping ceiling that ran up either side of the room seemed to ominously frame the door, which caused her to recall what she'd read in the dossier: that Nathaniel Barrow had made that space his own.

Does that mean he's in there now... waiting for me?

She had no intention of going in, intending just to wait

until she could figure out what to do. But then the door below her opened up. She almost cried as she shone her flashlight down and saw the man with the dangling eye climb onto the first step, the maid close behind him. They slowly made their way up.

Thud.

Thud.

Thud.

Their footfalls were slow but heavy.

Jodie knew she had nowhere else to go. She *had* to carry on deeper into the attic. Yet that was a dead end. Once in, she'd be trapped.

The roof windows again seemed the only escape.

Thud.

Thud.

Thud.

The two spirits continued their slow advance. Jodie backed up towards the door behind her. Once inside the attic, she would close the door behind her, though she no longer had any confidence that would stop her pursuers.

Thud, thud, thud.

The footsteps were faster now, the moans that drifted up distinctly excited. Jodie ran, taking the steps up to the door in one bound, grabbing the handle at the top. She attempted to push it open to flee inside... only, the door didn't budge.

What the hell?

She tried again, frantically shaking the handle and slamming her body against the door. Still nothing.

Nooo!

She couldn't understand why it wouldn't open. *There's no way it's locked, right?* The door didn't *seem* locked, yet it didn't even shake in its hinges when Jodie thrust herself against it. It didn't move at all, stuck fast, like a block of concrete.

She continued to ram her shoulder into the door, utterly

desperate, hearing the continual *thump, thump, thump* of rising footsteps. She turned and aimed her flashlight back towards the stairs just as the head of the man rose into view. He stumbled fully out into the vestibule, still followed closely by the maid, who shuffled next to him. Both slowly advanced, arms raised.

This can't be happening! This can't be happening!

'Get away from me!' Jodie screamed.

The man before her just smiled.

16

That's... *a person,* Joe thought to himself with a sinking realisation.

And the yelling voice… he'd heard it before. Earlier that night.

It can't be.

It was the woman. After hearing the cry of, 'Get away from me,' it had clicked in Joe's mind.

But... she left. I watched her go.

Joe wondered if the spirits could copy voices; perhaps this was just some kind of game to them, a way to unnerve him, or maybe lure him upstairs. Voice mimicry was not something he'd been briefed on, but he knew it wasn't an impossibility. Even so, his instinct told him this was *really* her.

The woman had come back.

'Damn it,' he seethed. *What the hell was she thinking?*

While he'd been threatening to her before, Joe had actually held back and tried not to be *too* much of a bully. That had been a mistake. He should have made absolutely certain she was too scared to return.

Because if she *had* come back, that was yet another failure on his part.

And, potentially, another death on his conscience to plague his nightmares.

Joe couldn't let that happen. Rushing upstairs would be foolhardy, but by the sound of it, the woman didn't have much time left.

Shit.

Joe took off running.

17

JODIE PRESSED HER BACK UP AGAINST THE DOOR AS THE TWO spirits approached. It was hard to think clearly, hard to come up with a plan of action. Her mind was just too clouded with fear.

She looked to the side of each ghost—there was space to run past them. But she then remembered how quickly the woman had moved on the stairs: scuttling up them at incredible speed. Jodie wondered if the space was being left to lure her into getting closer just so they could pounce.

Now even more desperate, Jodie turned and tried the door again, grabbing the handle and shaking it frantically.

'Come on!'

The spirits edged ever closer, almost within grabbing distance, arms raised, fingers twitching. Jodie drove her shoulder into the door once more, readying herself to be grabbed.

However… the door gave, suddenly swinging open, whatever had been stopping it now gone.

Jodie fell forward, totally unprepared for the lack of resistance, dropping her flashlight when she hit the ground. The device bounced against her heel and spun off into the vestibule area, rolling past the advancing spirits.

No!

Even more panic flooded her. She *needed* the light, but it was too close to the ghosts, with no way for her to get it without being caught.

With the spirits still advancing, Jodie knew she had to close the door and cut them off, flashlight in hand or not, so she quickly scrambled to her feet. Yet before she could even grab the handle, the door slammed shut on its own, plunging her into utter darkness.

What the hell?

She instinctively rushed to it and tried to open the door again, pulling at it frantically, not caring about the approaching horrors outside. She just needed to be out of the darkness.

But the door was stuck again. A sinking realisation washed over her—she'd been deliberately herded into the attic.

She pulled at the handle, twisting and yanking it. The door didn't budge.

Jodie couldn't hear the excited moans outside anymore. She couldn't hear anything. *Have they gone?*

Eventually, Jodie gave up. She slowly turned around, back still pressed tightly against the door behind her. In the surrounding darkness, she could see a hint of moonlight that slithered down through one of the roof windows, but it offered only a shard of dull light. Everything else was black.

The silence that had suddenly descended was almost unbearable, broken only by her own frantic breathing. Jodie couldn't explain why, but she got the overwhelming sensation that there was something in the attic with her: something out there in the dark. Somehow, she just *knew* it wasn't like the things she had seen so far in the building.

This... was something else.

Her shaking became uncontrollable. She thought through her options, but was interrupted when she heard a slow, laboured breath, the sound creeping out from the dark. Her body locked up and her heart seized. The strength in her legs vanished, leaving her weak and barely able to stay standing.

The slow breath came again, this time accompanied by a long, rattling exhalation. Jodie's sobs increased. Her fear spiked far beyond what she'd felt when the two spirits had been pursuing her up the stairs, though it was hard to explain why. This time, it was like she was being watched by some terrible, unseen being; she was a bug under a microscope, studied by something that could squash her in the blink of an eye.

Jodie narrowed her eyes in a vain attempt to see through the dark. It was no good. Her gaze then fell on the only thing she *could* see: the beam of moonlight that drifted down from one of the roof windows. As she looked at that... she *did* see something, at the back of the space, though it took her a moment to figure out just what she was looking at.

Eyes, she realised.

They looked to be around eight feet up in the air, though it was hard to be certain with no frame of reference.

The eyes weren't human, she had no doubt about that, and the only reason she could see them at all is because the red stood out against the darkness.

The red was dull and faint, just visible enough to make out. Even as she looked on, they slowly faded away, leaving only the shadows. Panic built even more within her.

Slow footsteps approached from the back of the room, drawing steadily closer. *Clomp. Clomp. Clomp.*

The breathing continued: a slow inhalation followed by a rattling exhale, over and over.

As Jodie stared at the shard of light, she soon saw a

person move close to it and stop. The figure was little more than a shadow, but Jodie could just make out what she thought was a shoulder and arm at the edge of the light. The breathing halted, and the person remained completely motionless.

Jodie slowly forced herself to turn and try to force the handle again.

Open. For the love of God, please open.

It didn't. Eyes wet with tears, she turned back—the shadow was gone. Jodie heard another breath.

But it was closer now.

Whatever was out there had advanced, without footsteps this time. Jodie pulled harder at the door.

Come on! Come on!

Jodie turned back. The shaft of light was gone, blocked out by something nearby. There was another breath. It was so close she felt it drift over her face while taking in its fetid stink. Jodie gasped and screamed, knowing the unseen entity was right in front of her now.

'Get away from me! Get away!'

She could barely move, body locked with fear. Even though she couldn't see anything, Jodie could *feel* it watching her, its gaze almost maddening. She wanted to swing a fist, to punch out at whatever was there, but was too scared. The thought of touching it horrified her.

Like it was responding to her thought, it touched *her*.

She felt a cold, clammy hand grab the side of her head and she screamed a second time at the feeling of fingers slithering their way into her mouth and pressing on her tongue.

'Hello?' came a voice from beyond the door. 'Is that you? What's going on?'

It was the stranger.

She tried to snap her head away from what held her, but

the grip on her was too tight; the fingers continued to slither farther into her mouth, probing at her throat, making her gag.

'Heeeeelgh!' Her cry for help was muffled, full of panic. The door started to rattle behind her.

'Open up!' he shouted. 'Open up and get out here! Now!'

I don't want to be *in here,* Jodie thought. She gagged again as the cold fingers started to wiggle. A hoarse voice came from in front of her as another wave of stink like rotted meat rolled forward.

'Sooooon.'

In an instant, Jodie was released, the thing that held her—and the fingers in her throat—suddenly gone. The door burst inwards at the same moment, striking Jodie and sending her sprawling forward to the floor.

She spun as she landed, arms raised as a blue light shone over her. She could see the form of the stranger behind the light.

'What the hell are you still *doing* here?' he demanded, glaring. His eyes met hers for a moment, but then they flicked up, searching the attic as he raised the lantern higher. 'What happened? Why were you screaming?'

Jodie didn't answer any of his questions. Instead, she found the strength to move again. She pushed herself to her feet and scrambled forward, forcing her way past the man to jump down the three steps and stumble into the vestibule, desperate to get away from the attic. She quickly spotted her flashlight, which she snatched up.

'Hey!' the man called from behind. 'I asked you a question. Why are you here?'

Jodie continued to run, using her flashlight to guide her as she sprinted back to the stairs, though she heard him following along behind.

'Hey!' the man called again.

'We need to get out of here!' she shouted back, breathless. 'There's something in there. In the attic! We need to get away.'

Jodie thundered down the stairs, images of the dead man with the dangling eye popping up in her mind, but she didn't care.

She didn't dare stop.

In truth, Jodie would happily face the man and the maid a dozen times if it meant avoiding the thing in the attic.

When Jodie was halfway down the stairs, she heard the man above thumping down as well.

'What is in the attic?' he shouted. 'What did you see?'

'We need to leave!' she shouted back as she raced into the function area.

She heard the stranger's rapid footsteps behind her, moving quickly.

Jodie kept going with the man closing in. She didn't know if he was running with her or chasing her—it felt like the latter.

'Wait!' he shouted, sounding entirely too close, his blue light washing over her and causing Jodie's shadow to stretch out across the floor in front of her. She continued to the door, ducking into the entrance hallway before rushing through and emerging into the old hall. After making it only a few steps inside, she felt a hand finally grab her shoulder.

Jodie tried to shrug it off, but the grip remained on her coat, yanking her backwards and spinning her around.

The stranger was there, a glare on his face. Jodie reacted angrily and pushed him. 'Get off me! I need to get out of here!'

Yet the man's grip didn't falter. 'Hold on a second,' he shouted. 'Just wait!' He looked angry himself. 'What the hell are you still doing here? You *left!*'

Jodie took a moment, teeth clenched, still terrified. 'I… came back,' she eventually replied.

'Why?'

'Because I fucking wanted to!' Jodie shouted. 'Because I didn't want to be pushed around.' She then gazed over his shoulder to the dark beyond him, imagining the thing from the attic following. 'But it was a mistake,' she admitted. 'So… I'm leaving. For good this time.' Her eyes then met his. 'You should go too. You can't stay here. It's dangerous.'

The man hesitated. 'I know,' he eventually said.

'You… know?' Jodie asked. 'What do you mean, you know?'

'What did you see up in the attic?' the man went on, ignoring her response.

'I didn't *see* anything,' she shot back. 'It was too dark. I… felt something, though.' Jodie's hands came up and touched her mouth. A pang of anger surged up. 'And I felt it put its fucking fingers in my mouth,' she snarled. 'It tried to choke me.'

She also remembered what it had said.

Soooon.

'Shit,' the other man said with a sigh, looking down. He shook his head in annoyance. 'You need to get out of here.'

'I *know!*' Jodie shouted. 'I was *trying* to until you stopped me.'

'But… there's a problem with that,' the man said. 'The presence in this place… it knows you're here, so—'

'No shit.'

'Let me finish,' he snapped. 'It knows you're here, so I doubt it will just let you walk away. It's feeding off you now, off us both.'

Jodie frowned. 'What the hell does that mean?'

He shook his head. 'It's… hard to explain.'

'I don't care,' Jodie said as she finally shrugged off his hold. 'I'm going, I've had enough.'

She turned to move to the open window but stopped with a gasp. There was a hand on the windowsill, gripping the edge, skin pale with black fingernails. The fingers slowly wiggled.

Jodie quickly turned to the other side of the room, and just as her eyes fell on one of the windows there she spotted a shadowy figure quickly pull back out of sight. Her breath caught in her throat.

'How… how many of those things are out there?'

'To be honest, I don't know,' the man replied. 'But they want to keep us here. If you go outside…'

'If I go outside… *what,* exactly?' Jodie demanded.

'Then I don't know what will happen,' the man replied. 'But it would be dangerous.'

'And staying inside *isn't?*'

The stranger nodded. 'It is, but I know the force here will do whatever it can to stop you from leaving the grounds.'

Force?

'What's going on?' Jodie demanded. 'How do you know so much about it all?'

It didn't seem like he was listening, as he looked to the side, clearly thinking. '*That's* why I didn't see as much activity as I expected,' he said in realisation, ignoring Jodie's question completely. 'It was focused on *you.*'

Jodie glanced over at the hand again, just in time to see it slowly snake backwards and disappear beneath the sill.

'I need you to tell me what's going on. Seriously,' Jodie said, trying to keep her voice calm and assertive.

The other man studied her, then shook his head. 'I'm afraid I can't tell you a lot. And also, if I do manage to get you out of this, I'm gonna need you to 'forget' everything that happened here. That's non-negotiable. You forget it and don't tell a soul.'

Jodie wanted to argue, wanted to ask if that was a threat, but ultimately, she knew it would do no good. And besides, *who* was she going to tell? Tony would be furious with her, and what was more, she had a feeling he'd want to pry into the events and investigate for himself, which would obviously lead to more trouble.

'I won't tell a soul,' she said. 'I wouldn't want to.'

'I need you to promise me,' the man said. 'It's impo—'

'I promise,' Jodie quickly interjected, her eyes constantly flicking back and forth between the man and the windows. 'I won't say a thing. I swear it. So… please… just help me get away.'

The man continued to study her. 'I will,' he eventually said with a nod. 'But… we won't be able to just yet.'

'What?! Why?'

'Because it'll do no good,' the man stated. 'The things here… they won't let us leave, like I said. We have to finish what I started. After that, you'll be free.'

'I… I don't know what you're talking about,' Jodie answered, sounding as desperate as she felt. She just wanted to be free of the building. 'What did you start here? None of this is making sense.'

The man sighed. 'What's your name?'

'Why?'

He rolled his eyes. 'So I know what to call you.'

Jodie felt uncomfortable giving her name away, and was tempted to tell him a false one, but in the end, he was the only help she had. 'Jodie,' she admitted. 'Yours?'

'Joe,' he said. 'Nice to meet you, Jodie.' She cocked an eyebrow as if to say, *that's bullshit*. He sighed again and went on, 'I'll tell you as much as I'm comfortable sharing, but it still isn't going to explain everything. You're just going to have to deal with that.'

'Okay,' Jodie said. She glanced at the window again. 'But first, shouldn't we uh… move somewhere else, given those things outside?'

'Those things are everywhere,' the man replied, raising his lamp and letting the blue glow wash over a wider area. 'This space is probably as safe as any for now, I suppose. Nothing I can see hiding in the shadows.'

'But the things outside—'

'Are there to keep us in here,' Joe explained. 'So the dark entity can keep feeding.'

'What do you mean when you say that?' Jodie asked. She wasn't familiar with that term. 'Dark entity? Do you just mean a malevolent ghost?'

Joe shook his head. 'No, it's more than that. Far more. What we're dealing with here is like an oni, or dark kami… kind of. You familiar with what an oni is?'

'They're Japanese, right?' Jodie replied. 'Demons or spirits or something.'

'Kind of,' Joe said, as he scratched the back of his neck. 'They're part of the Shinto religion, which is Japanese originally, so you got that part right. But the religion extends far beyond just Japan. And these things are more than just spirits. I suppose the closest thing you might compare them to is a demon, but again, that's not exactly right. They exist because of energies. And a place like this, well, it's built up *a lot* of negative energy over the years. When that happens, sometimes certain… *things…* take hold. Those things then grow and fester.'

'And the ghosts here are all… oni?'

Joe shook his head. 'First, what I'm talking about isn't the same as an oni. Not quite. Plus, there's only one dark entity here. The other spirits are just ensnared by it, trapped and used like puppets.'

It was a lot for Jodie to take in, yet one thing in particular jumped out as not making sense. 'Wait,' she began. 'Surely there would have been more stories about the hall, if that thing is so bad. I mean, the things I've seen here tonight… no way they happened to other people too. Zero chance. We would have heard about it.'

'That's true,' the man said. 'Before tonight, all activity would have just seemed like a normal haunting, though maybe a *little* more insidious than usual. The tainted spirits still existed here. They don't tend to have a huge amount of power in our world, since there is a divide they can't fully break.'

'Well, they seemed to have broken it tonight,' Jodie said.

'That's right.'

'But… why tonight, specifically?' Then realisation hit. '*You* caused it!'

The man cocked his head to the side and narrowed his eyes. 'How do you figure?'

She noticed he hadn't denied it. 'That thing you were doing,' she went on. 'In the circle of stones. You were talking… if I had to guess it was in Japanese, with what you told me. What was it? A ritual?'

'You saw that?' he asked, his surprise obvious. 'How?'

'I… was up there,' she said, pointing to the mezzanine floor above. Joe's eyes followed. He sighed again.

'Aren't you a sneaky one. Yes, it was a ritual.'

'So… you summoned the thing here on *purpose?*'

'I didn't summon it, exactly,' Joe said. 'It was already here, like I said. But the ritual brings it through, opens the door, and allows the entity to manifest—as long as there are living things for it to feed on, of course.'

'Why on earth would you want to do that?!' Jodie asked, eyes wide with shock and anger.

Joe hesitated. 'That part doesn't matter,' he said. He looked again to the mezzanine. 'What exactly were you doing up there when you were watching me?'

'What do you mean?' Jodie asked.

'I mean… were you just watching? Or were you… recording?'

Now it was Jodie's turn to hesitate. 'I… recording,' she admitted. 'I wanted to know what you were up to. I wanted evidence.' She drew out her phone. 'Not that it matters. This thing died anyway.' She shook it in her hand. 'I don't think I got much.'

'Your phone is fucked,' the man stated. 'Might as well get a new one. It won't work anymore. But I'm concerned the video you took might have uploaded somewhere.' He narrowed his eyes before continuing. 'Though thinking about it, there shouldn't have been a signal.'

'What do you mean?' Jodie asked. 'Why did my phone die? What happened?'

'Did you feel anything while I was performing the ritual? Like a wave wash over you?'

'Yes,' Jodie said. 'That's when my phone cut out.'

Joe nodded. 'I figured. It's kind of like an electrical pulse.'

'An EMP?'

'Similar… but not the same,' Joe said. 'Spirits and energies do carry electrical charges… of a sort. That pulse fried the circuits in your phone.'

'But my flashlight still works,' Jodie said, waving it in front of her.

The man's eyes fell on it. 'Was it off when the pulse hit?'

Jodie nodded. 'Yeah, it was.'

'That's a big part of why. It looks like an old flashlight as well. Sturdy, but not an LED. I'm guessing just a flip switch and batteries, with little else inside?'

Jodie looked at the flashlight herself. 'I… have no idea. I've had it for years.'

'Well, if it was a newer, more high-tech one, it would have been fried as well. The fact it isn't is a stroke of luck for you. Otherwise, you'd have been stumbling around in complete darkness.'

'And that's why you use… *that?*' Jodie said, pointing to the lantern.

'One of the reasons,' Joe said. 'But there's more to it. Look, when we're safe, I'm going to need to make sure that video didn't upload to cloud storage. I need to be certain. I can't have video footage of me leaking out.'

'I won't leak anything,' Jodie said.

'Afraid I can't just take your word on that, Jodie,' Joe replied. 'I trust you enough not to go blabbing, because even if you do, you'd have no real proof. But footage is—'

'There won't be any footage,' Jodie said. 'My phone was set to upload only with Wi-Fi signal, which we don't have here. So nothing got out before the pulse. Trust me, that video died with my phone.'

Joe continued to look at her. 'We'll see,' was all he said.

There was a moment's silence, which Jodie soon decided to fill. 'Are you working alone?' she asked, voicing a question that had been on her mind since she saw him perform the ritual.

'Of course,' the man said. 'There's no one here with me other than you.'

Jodie quickly shook her head, realising she'd phrased it incorrectly. 'No, I mean, are you alone in what you do? That'—she pointed to the lantern—'the ritual, the stuff you know… are you on a one-man mission, or are you part of a group?' He didn't respond. 'A group, then,' Jodie went on. 'I figured as much. Just *who* are you guys?'

'I can't say,' Joe replied. 'In truth, there's a lot I don't know, but I've also told you pretty much all I can. I'm not comfortable saying more.'

'Well… you're going to *have* to give me more. I mean, you said the only way to survive was to see through what you started, right? What was it you started? What are you doing here and how long until it's finished?'

There was another pause before he replied, 'I don't know how long exactly, but we need to wait until the dark spirit fully manifests.'

'Is that what I saw up in the attic?' she asked. 'The thing that stuck its fingers in my throat? It felt… different from the others, somehow. Darker. Being around it was just… just…' She didn't know how to finish the sentence.

'Yeah, that's it alright,' Joe said. 'That's Nathaniel Barrow.'

'*He's* the dark spirit?' Jodie asked. 'I thought you said it was an… an energy or something?'

'It is, but that energy latches on to spirits,' Joe said. 'His actions would have created it over the years, and when he died, it consumed him. He's one with it now.'

'Jesus,' Jodie said. 'That's a horrible existence. Not that he deserved any better, I suppose.'

'He doesn't, but the other spirits here *do* deserve better. Though they're stuck here, controlled by the dark.'

'Is that why you're doing all this?' Jodie asked. 'To set them free?'

There was yet another pause. 'That's right,' Joe said.

Jodie instantly knew that was a lie. However, she didn't want to press things. Ultimately, it wasn't important—surviving was the only thing that mattered.

'So, how *do* you set them free?' she asked. 'And how do we end what's happening? Do we have to exorcise the oni?'

Joe shook his head. 'No, we don't. We trap it. Then we take it away from this place.'

'Trap it?' Jodie asked, confused. 'That… doesn't make any sense. You can't *trap* a ghost… can you?'

'Trap a *dark spirit,*' Joe corrected. 'And yes, you can. Well, you imprison it. Then it can be safely removed.'

'Imprison it?' Jodie was having a hard time believing what he was telling her. She was open to a lot of things in life—hell, she'd dedicated a good portion of hers hunting ghosts, something many people scoffed at.

But this…

'Seriously?' she asked. 'You just send these things to… what… ghost prison? How does that even work?'

'It doesn't matter,' Joe said. 'When the time comes, I'll take care of it, and until then, just keep close and stay out of danger.'

'Will staying close to you actually *keep* me out of danger, Joe?' Jodie asked.

'I… I guess not,' he admitted. 'But it's better than wandering around on your own or trying to get away outside.'

Jodie sighed. 'So, what do we do until the time is right? Do we just… wait and let that thing keep feeding off us?'

'Afraid so,' Joe said.

'That doesn't sound like a great option.'

'It's our only option.'

Jodie wanted to curse in frustration, or shout, or hit something, just to do *something*. She gazed out of the window once more. It was like a cruel joke, having an exit so close but knowing she couldn't use it—freedom was dangling yet was just out of reach.

'What happens when that thing feeds?' Jodie went on. 'I don't feel anything weird happening. Will it feeding make us weaker or hurt us?'

Joe shook his head. 'Maybe 'feed' was the wrong word,' he said. 'But I just didn't know how else to explain it. It uses us as a kind of anchor point, or magnet, to hold it here as it fully comes through. It needs living energy to hone in on. Does that make sense?'

'*Nothing* about what you're saying makes sense,' Jodie said, then paused. 'But I think I follow.' She narrowed her eyes. 'And there's nothing else you can tell me that might be of use?'

Joe shook his head. 'Not that I can think of. I've given you plenty already.'

'Well, it still feels like there are a lot of holes in what you're telling me.'

He gave her a sympathetic smile. 'If it means anything, there are plenty of holes for me too.'

'Why?' Jodie asked. 'You new at this or something?' He didn't answer, instead looking away. 'Wait… you are!' she said with realisation. 'This… this is your first time, isn't it?'

'It doesn't matter,' Joe stated flatly.

'It matters plenty,' Jodie replied, feeling her nerves rise once again. 'You mean to tell me you've never actually trapped one of these things before? How do you even know it will work?'

'It'll work.'

'But how do you *know?*'

'Because I just do!' Joe snapped. 'Now just stop asking questions, alright? I'm the only chance you have here so just… let me work.'

Yet again, Jodie wanted to push back, and yet again she held off. If what the man was saying was true, and she was inclined to believe him, then he was right: he was her best chance of survival. Which meant it wasn't a good idea to piss him off.

'Fair enough,' she eventually replied. 'I'll follow your lead.

But please, Joe, don't fuck this up. I really, *really* don't want to die.'

'Me neither,' he said with a forced smile. 'But don't worry, I've been in worse situations than this and made it out.'

'Really?' she asked with a cocked eyebrow.

'Yes,' he said. Yet his hesitation left Jodie not quite sure she believed him.

18

Joe battled to keep a lid on his frustrations.

Though unintentional, the woman had put her life in jeopardy and made his mission infinitely more difficult. Now, not only did he have to survive until the time was right, he had to make sure *she* survived as well.

His consciousness couldn't take another death that was his fault.

The pair slowly walked down the corridor, with Joe holding out his lantern to light the way. Jodie had switched off her flashlight, as it was rendered moot by the lamp.

'I have a question,' Joe said as they walked. He'd noticed how anxious she was, how on edge, and hoped a little conversation might help dull her fear.

'What?' she asked.

'What's your interest in this place? I mean, you know why *I'm* here—at least, you know some of it—but I still don't get why you would come in the middle of the night. You a ghost hunter or something?'

'Bingo,' she said. 'How'd you know?'

'I didn't, really,' Joe replied. 'It was just a wild guess. All I could think of. You often go ghost hunting alone?'

'No... not really,' the woman admitted. 'This is actually my first time going solo. It'll be my last as well.'

'So why now, then?' he asked. 'And why this place?'

'It was recently abandoned,' Jodie replied. 'First time in a long while I had the opportunity to get back in.'

'*Back* in? You've been here before?'

Jodie gave a slow nod. 'Yeah. A while ago, before the most recent owners took possession.'

'Then you must have seen something really good, if it made you want to come back.'

'Yeah,' Jodie said. 'Yeah, we did.'

'And who is the 'we'? Friends of yours?'

'It doesn't matter,' the woman replied. 'I don't want to talk about it.'

Joe narrowed his eyes at her, sensing he'd struck a nerve. 'Come on,' he pressed. 'I won't say anything. You can trust me.' She turned her eyes to him, shooting over a doubtful look. 'Who am I going to tell? What you did here back then has no bearing on me.'

The woman took a moment. 'I was here with my friend and my husband,' she eventually said. 'Well, he was my boyfriend at the time.'

'And why aren't they here tonight?' Joe asked.

'My friend wouldn't approve,' Jodie said. 'He isn't big on breaking into places. He likes doing things above the line.'

'Makes sense. But what about your husband? Is he okay with you being here?'

Another pause, this one much longer. 'He's dead,' the woman eventually said.

'Oh,' Joe replied after a moment, having been taken by surprise. 'I'm... sorry.'

The woman shrugged. 'It is what it is. He actually

proposed when we were here, so the building is…' She trailed off.

'It's special?' Joe asked and Jodie nodded. 'Then it's making more sense why you came back here.' He almost kept going and told Jodie about Gemma, but refrained at the last moment. 'So what happened back then?' he questioned instead. 'Other than the proposal?'

'We were doing a Ouija board session, and—' Jodie began.

'Those work?' Joe interjected with a cocked eyebrow. 'I thought those things were just toys.'

'No, the idea was around long before some toy company came along and made a board game out of it.'

'And… they actually get results?'

'They can,' Jodie said. 'Though they are easily manipulated. We were doing a session with it up in the attic when… things started happening. The lights we had with us started going nuts, flashing and strobing, then the board flipped over. I even saw a figure standing there with us.'

'Jesus,' Joe uttered. 'That's… pretty intense. You see much of that kind of thing being a ghost hunter?'

Jodie shook her head. 'No, that was one of the more extreme events. Actually, the most-extreme event I've seen while hunting, not counting tonight.'

Joe looked around the corridor and whistled. 'The energy here must be really strong, then. That's good to know.'

'Why?' Jodie asked. 'Has it really given you any great insight?'

Joe nodded. 'If it was powerful enough to cause that back then, then we're *really* going to have to be on our guard.'

'That doesn't make me feel any better.'

Joe laughed. 'Sorry. Scaring you wasn't my intent, though. Just emphasising that we need to be ready.'

'I'm about as ready as I can be. I don't think I've ever been this on edge.'

'Well, try to keep everything in check,' Joe said. 'Don't get me wrong, that nervous energy is useful—critical, even—but it can also get the better of you if you let it.'

'I thought you said you hadn't done this kind of thing before? How do you know so much about 'nervous energy'?'

'I just... do,' Joe replied.

He could feel her looking at him. 'Military, right?' she said, taking him by surprise. 'At least, *former* military.'

He turned to her. 'How did you know?'

Jodie smiled. 'I didn't. Just a wild guess. Though you do carry yourself a certain way. It made me think military.'

'Guess you have a keen eye.'

'So... what branch of the military?' Jodie questioned. 'Army, navy, S.A.S?'

'Army,' Joe replied.

'Were you a soldier for a long time?'

He nodded. 'Signed up straight after school. Only retired from it last year.'

'And how did you get caught up with... whatever you're involved in now?'

He shifted uncomfortably and hesitated. 'I don't want to talk about it.'

'I didn't want to talk about my husband,' Jodie was quick to say, 'but I did.' Yet Joe stayed silent. He heard the woman's sigh to his side. 'Fine,' she said.

As they reached the end of the corridor, Jodie turned her head and looked back at the bank of windows, staring longingly.

'Thinking of making a break for it?' Joe asked.

'I dunno,' she said. 'It looks inviting. There's a lot of space out there, and I'm not in terrible shape. Just wondering if I could outpace whatever came after me.'

'Well, I can't stop you from trying,' Joe said. 'It's not like I'm holding you prisoner here. But... I wouldn't advise it.'

'You think it's a death sentence going out there, don't you?'

'Maybe,' Joe said. 'This *is* my first rodeo, as you know, but from what I understand... yeah, let's just say I don't think it would be safe.'

'Being in here isn't safe either.'

'But being out there would be worse.'

'Are you certain?'

Joe shrugged. 'I'm not certain about *any* of this. But I know what I've been told, and I know what my instincts are saying. I honestly don't think you'll just be able to outrun whatever is here.' The woman continued to look over at the window. 'It's your call,' Joe went on. 'I won't stop you.'

'Why don't you come with me?' Jodie asked, turning to him.

'What do you mean?'

'We can both make a run for it, get out together. Just forget what you're doing here, forget the whole stupid thing. Let's just... go.'

Joe shook his head. 'I can't leave this unfinished, trust me,' he said. 'If I do, the building won't be safe for anyone in the future. Leaving just... isn't an option for me.'

A frown crept over her face. 'Because what you've unleashed will still be here?'

'Right,' he said.

Another sigh. 'Joe, that's... do you have any idea how reckless your whole mission is? You can't... you can't just do things like that, not when they could affect other people so much. Jesus Christ, who on Earth do you work for?'

'I said to drop it,' Joe stated, calmly but forcefully. 'I mean it.'

The woman gazed at him long and hard. 'All this so you can save the trapped spirits, right?' It was clear she didn't believe a word of what he'd said.

'That's right,' he replied. 'Now, I'm gonna need you to stop with both the questions and the judgement, alright? I need to focus.'

Jodie stayed quiet for a moment. 'Fine,' she eventually said. 'But you better accomplish your goal. And then you can go back and tell your bosses that what they're doing isn't right.' It looked like she was going to follow up with something, but she stayed quiet.

'Don't worry, I'll be sure to tell them,' Joe said sarcastically.

'So... what now?' Jodie asked. 'Do we just keep walking aimlessly?'

She folded her arms across her chest and Joe was instantly reminded of Gemma. It was her defensive pose, used whenever she disagreed with him.

Jodie didn't look like Joe's wife had, of course—Jodie was a brunette, whereas Gemma was a redhead, and Gemma was shorter and stockier. But both women had similar attitudes, similar auras, and both were evidently happy to bite back when they saw things that weren't right. And that endeared Jodie to him, as frustrating as her questions were.

For the briefest moment, Joe wondered if she was single. He had a passing thought of asking, but quickly quashed the idea, scolding himself.

Gemma is all that counts.

A sudden self-loathing came over him in a wave, guilt for momentarily forgetting his purpose.

He eventually responded to her question. 'Yeah, we kind of do just keep walking. Nothing else to do until things progress.'

'Okay,' Jodie said. 'And... how will we know when it's done? You know, the manifestation thing?'

'Don't worry, we'll know,' Joe said. He wiggled the

lantern. 'This will give us a tell.' He then reached into his pocket and drew out the shard compass. 'As will this.'

He saw the woman cock her head to the side. 'A compass?'

'Yeah, but a modified one,' he replied.

'Why is it moving like that?' Jodie asked. 'Is it broken? It's just... spinning.'

Joe watched the shard and noticed that while its rotations were still slow, they were faster than before, indicative of the increased activity in the building.

'Because there is a lot going on around us,' he replied.

Jodie leaned in closer to the object. 'What's with the needle? It doesn't look like a regular one. It's jagged, like black glass.'

'It doesn't matter,' Joe said. 'All that *does* matter is that it will alert us when things are done.' He pocketed the implement once more.

'Then why don't you continue holding it so you can keep an eye on it?'

He wiggled the lantern again. 'This will be enough. Plus, I want to keep at least one hand free in case I need it.'

'Strange toys you have there,' Jodie said with a raised eyebrow.

'What, like ghost hunters don't have toys?'

'Well... yeah. But we use more traditional things. EVP readers, video and audio recorders, heat cameras, that sort of thing... not blue lanterns and old compasses. Don't you use the regular stuff?'

'I have things like that with me, sure,' Joe said. 'But in all honesty, they won't show me anything the lantern won't.'

The woman stared at the lamp, leaning in a little, looking at the flame inside. 'Why does it burn that colour?'

'I can't divulge that,' Joe said, hiding that he simply didn't know. Though he couldn't help but be amused at how fascinated she was with it.

Joe briefly considered showing her the echo glass as well, curious what she would make of that. He imagined it would be of great interest. But ultimately he refrained, wanting to hold back as much as he could. She'd seen the lantern already, and it would have only been a matter of time for the compass, since he'd need to use it at some point anyway.

She would no doubt see the soul vessel, but he didn't want to reveal more than he had to. For now, he just needed to keep moving.

'Come on,' he eventually said. 'We might as well continue on. I don't feel comfortable just standing in one spot like this.'

'If we have to,' Jodie said. 'It's just… hard. I keep feeling that things are going to jump out at us out of nowhere. I hate it.'

'The lantern will help with that,' Joe said. 'A lot of the time, when we think they're just jumping out of nowhere, they've actually been hiding and waiting. They're actually there, but outside of what we can see, cloaked by the veil. But the lantern can show them, push back the shadows and reveal what's lurking.'

'Really?' Jodie asked, staring at the tool again. 'How?'

'Doesn't matter,' Joe said. 'But just know that if anything *has* come through, this will force it into the light.' He held the lantern higher to cast its glow farther, as if illustrating his point. He made a show of slowly turning about in a circle, forcing the shadows back.

Just as he'd completed a half circle, Joe froze. The lantern revealed a ghost standing stock-still about twenty feet away, watching them with wide eyes.

Jodie screamed.

19

WITH HER HANDS TO HER MOUTH, JODIE STUMBLED BACKWARDS away from the spirit—the same one from earlier, with the dirty overalls and dangling eye. He stood motionless farther down the hallway, just at the edge of the lantern's light. However, as the light touched the spirit, it turned its head away, lifting up a protective hand. The man then inched backwards a couple of paces.

Jodie's terrified mind instantly questioned how long he'd been standing there watching them. *He was so close.*

'It's okay,' Joe said, holding a protective arm in front of Jodie.

'*How* is it okay?' Jodie asked, louder and more panicked than she would have liked.

'Just move back slowly,' the man said, pushing himself into Jodie and forcing her to step backward with him.

'Can it hurt us?' Jodie asked, staring at the entity with wide eyes.

'Yes,' Joe simply stated.

The spirit continued to shield itself from the glow of the

lamp, and while Jodie remained terrified, it was a relief the lantern appeared to offer them protection.

'Will the light keep it away?'

'For a while,' Joe said. 'They don't like it.' As she moved with Joe, Jodie saw the entity take a tentative step forward, still shielding its face but pushing itself through whatever pain or discomfort it was experiencing. In response, Joe took a big step forward himself, holding the lantern out before him. The spirit snarled and halted its movement, then retreated back again. Joe took another step, pushing it back farther.

'Wanna try again?' Joe called over to the spirit, challenging it. In response, the entity just slunk back even more, soon becoming lost in the deeper shadows of the corridor.

After a moment, Joe pulled out his compass. Jodie stared at its glass front, seeing the jagged needle pointing straight ahead. To her surprise, it was glowing, though the blue-white hue was quickly fading. Eventually, the colour drained completely.

'It's gone,' Joe said.

'Are... are you sure?' Jodie still felt tense, and she had to fight to stop from clinging to the man for protection.

'As sure as I can be,' Joe said. 'Doesn't mean it won't come back, though.'

Jodie turned and looked to the door ahead, which they had been walking towards. 'Maybe it's just through there.'

Joe shook his head. 'The compass would have picked it up,' he said.

'But you had the compass out before, and it didn't say anything was behind us then,' Jodie replied, uneasy.

'Because nothing *was* behind us then,' Joe answered. 'The compass will only show things that have come through the veil. Same as the lantern. But once they pull back, well...

there's nothing to show.' He looked to her. 'I know that might not make a lot of sense.'

'I—I don't know how much more of this I can take,' Jodie said, fighting to keep from sobbing. Her nerves felt like they were shot, her energy sapped after so many scares.

'You can take more than you think,' Joe said to her. 'Find a way to fight through the fear, Jodie. It's possible, believe me. And you're gonna *have* to do it, understand?' His tone wasn't harsh, but it certainly wasn't kind. He was challenging her. She understood that. She also knew why he was doing it—because he couldn't afford for her to become dead weight.

And she couldn't afford that either.

She then thought back again to what had happened at her grandma's. *You've been this scared before,* Jodie reminded herself. *And you fought through it, even though you were just a child.*

'Can I count on you?' Joe went on to ask.

Jodie took a moment, but eventually gave a firm nod. 'Y—yeah,' she said, though her voice cracked. She coughed. 'Yes,' she said again, this time more firmly. 'You can count on me.' She straightened her posture and balled her fists, almost *willing* her strength to return.

'Good,' Joe said and put a hand on her shoulder. 'Stay close and stay alert. Two sets of eyes are better than one.' He made to move his arm down to his pocket, hesitated, then continued; he drew out the compass. 'Here,' he said, handing it over. 'Keep an eye on that and shout if it glows or focuses in one direction.'

Cautiously, Jodie took it, looking down at the device. It looked old. *Really* old. So, she handled it with care. 'Okay,' she said, feeling better at actually having a purpose. *Why do I get the feeling that was his intention?*

'Just don't break it,' Joe said. 'I don't know how replaceable these toys are, so just... be careful.'

'I will.' She looked at the glass screen to see the obsidian shard rotating as it had before, and while staring, she couldn't help wonder what material the needle was actually made of.

Joe turned and moved on, leading Jodie closer to the door. Jodie kept alternating her focus, glancing between the compass and the way forward. Every so often, she also looked behind as well. The compass wasn't showing anything, though she couldn't help but feel like they were being followed.

'Why do you like to keep on the move, anyway?' Jodie asked as they neared the door. 'Wouldn't sitting in one spot be an easier way to pass the time?'

'Not really,' Joe said. 'Though it would be an easier way for something to hone in on you. It's not like the things here don't know we're in the building; if we're stationary, we're an easier target to find and attack. If we're moving, at least we're harder to keep track of. Hopefully.'

'Hopefully?'

Joe nodded. 'Yeah. I can't be certain about any of it, like I said, but it's what my gut is telling me.'

'From your army training?'

'That's right,' he replied. 'It's rare that staying put is better than being on the move. Plus, I find it's easier to handle the nerves if I'm doing something.'

'Wait... *you're* nervous?' Jodie asked in surprise.

'Of course,' he replied.

'But I thought... I dunno, I just assumed you wouldn't be. Because of, you know...'

'Being in the military,' Joe finished, sounding amused.

'Well... yeah. I'm sure you've seen some things.'

'Not everyone that serves has seen things. I have... but that doesn't stop me from being scared. It just helps me overcome the fear and deal with it. So right now, yeah, I'm scared. Plus, ghosts are a new kind of threat for me.'

'Fair point,' Jodie said. 'I guess you're not going to be able to shoot your way out of trouble here.'

'The military isn't all about 'shooting your way out of trouble', Jodie,' Joe said—Jodie's eyes went wide and her face flushed.

'Oh, no, I didn't mean it like that. I just meant…' She trailed off.

Joe chuckled. 'Relax, I know what you meant. I'm only teasing. But thinking about it, this is more your area of expertise, given what we're dealing with.'

'*Mine?*'

'Of course.' Joe put his hand on the door, opened it, then went through first, keeping the lantern high. 'I'm guessing you know a thing or two about ghosts, right?'

Jodie nodded. 'I guess. But this is still… different.'

'How long have you been investigating them?'

'A *long* time,' she replied. 'I kind of felt it was a calling.'

'And you've no doubt built up a fair knowledge in that time, right?'

'I like to think so.'

'Perfect. Then you're probably more well-versed in this than I am.'

Jodie appreciated the sentiment, as well as the attempt to bolster her confidence, but she knew this was *nothing* like what she was used to. 'Can't say I have any experience going against a dark spirit, though,' she said. 'Before tonight, I didn't even know they were a thing.'

As the pair entered the living room, Joe replied, 'Yeah, I understand that,' he said. 'But I'm guessing there's gotta be some crossover, right? I mean, in all honesty, until recently I thought ghosts and things like that were all bullshit, just something people clung to because they were afraid of death.'

'So I'm guessing being sent on this job changed that for you?'

The man paused before answering. 'No, it was something *before* that.' Jodie picked up on the man's change in tone. He sounded sad, almost... longing.

'What happened?' she asked.

But Joe shook his head. 'Don't worry about it. Anyway, my point was, all the stuff you know is probably still useful.'

Jodie wasn't sure she agreed with that. 'I guess we'll see,' she said. She *did* know a lot about the supernatural, but all of that knowledge was based on the prevailing theories within the paranormal community. The thing was, they didn't have any hard data or empirical proof to back up most of their ideas. Nothing was scientific fact.

They continued to look around the space, which was pointless in Jodie's mind: it was bare, with very little to look at and nothing she hadn't seen already. As they walked, she felt her foot shift in her left boot a little—the laces were starting to come undone. She thought about fixing it, but just as she started to tell Joe she needed a quick pause, she took in some floating dust in a breath and coughed. Her throat felt hoarse and scratchy.

'You okay?' Joe asked.

'Thirsty,' she replied. 'And my water bottle is back in the car.'

Joe smiled, then retrieved a metal flask from his hip. He held it out to her and shook it, liquid sloshing inside. 'Here,' he said. She stared at it. 'It's just water,' he went on.

Jodie smiled and took it gratefully. 'Thank you.' She unscrewed the lid, didn't bother wiping, and took a couple of small sips. While she could have happily drank more, she didn't want to be greedy and guzzle all the man's water.

She then handed the flask back.

'You want some more?' Joe asked.

Jodie shook her head. 'No, that's fine for now. Thank you.' She looked around. 'Where next? Isn't there anything specific we can be doing to help with trapping that thing when the time comes?'

Joe shook his head. 'Not really.'

'Nothing that we can search for, maybe to learn more about Nathaniel?'

'Why would that help?' Joe asked.

Jodie shrugged. 'No idea. I just feel like we should be doing *something*, you know?'

'I get it,' Joe said. 'That feeling of restlessness... I understand it all too well. But we just need to make sure we're ready to act when the time comes. The people that briefed me made it clear a lot can happen in this period. The entities around here don't have to kill us. They can hurt us, incapacitate us, get us as close to death as possible without finishing the job—all so the dark entity can keep feeding. We just need to hold out.'

Jodie nodded. 'Didn't the document in your car say something about the building being the anchor? What does that mean?'

Joe cocked an eyebrow. 'You read my dossier?'

Jodie felt herself go red. *Oh shit*. 'I... might have,' she admitted. 'After I snuck back.'

The man sighed and shook his head. 'Jesus, I've been careless,' he said. 'Not exactly a ringing endorsement for my first mission.'

'I won't tell anyone, don't worry,' Jodie said. 'But... what does it mean by anchor? I thought *we* were the anchors?'

Joe took a breath. 'A living presence is required to draw out a dark spirit in the first place. But the building being the anchor... that's different. The building is what actually ties the spirit to our world, confining it to its boundaries. And while the anchor doesn't *have* to be a building, from what I understand, it often is. It has to be something that is important to the corrupted spirit, something that meant a lot to it in life.'

'So all dark spirits have these… anchors?' Jodie asked.

'I'm saying too much here, Jodie. You really can't know any of this,' Joe said, turning his head away. 'Let's just focus on what we're doing.'

Jodie sighed and looked down, where her attention was quickly drawn to her compass. The shard was starting to emit a low hue. 'Erm… Joe?'

'I see it,' he replied. The shard rotated once more before settling in one direction, aiming back at the door the pair had just entered through. She looked ahead, but couldn't see anything in the doorway, despite the light from the lantern. *Whatever is out there is too far away to see right now,* she thought.

There was another door in the room, and that accessed a small utility room. The utility space had a rear door leading outside, but Jodie knew that exit was locked up tight.

The utility room *did* have a window, though.

'Why don't we go through there?' Jodie whispered, pointing to the utility door. 'See if we can get out of the building through the window.'

But Joe shook his head. 'The window is too small,' he said. 'And the back door is locked. We'd only end up trapping ourselves. Besides, like I keep telling you, we can't go outside.'

'Then what do we *do?*' she asked, panic rising, eyes on the compass.

Joe started to slowly walk towards the door. 'Stay close,' he said.

'Don't,' Jodie replied, reaching out a shaking hand to grab him. Joe turned his head over his shoulder to look at her.

'Remember what I said about managing fear,' he stated.

'The glow isn't as strong as it could be'—he nodded down to the compass—'so pull it together and let's see what we're dealing with.'

Jodie gritted her teeth and reluctantly went with him. *Ghost,* she thought to herself. *We're dealing with ghosts. Ghosts that want to hurt us. What more is there to find out?*

But she knew he was right about her needing to handle fear better.

Jodie inched up onto tip toes to peer over Joe's shoulder. Despite the light from the lantern, she couldn't see anything in the hallway ahead. She also glanced up the staircase to her immediate left as they exited the room; there, she could see up to the half-landing, which was all clear as well. Jodie checked the compass again to see it was pointing straight ahead.

No, she realised, *not quite.* It was angled slightly to the right, aiming more at the side wall of the corridor. *Something outside, maybe?*

She moved herself to Joe's side, closer to the stairs, ready to bolt up them if needed. 'There,' Joe suddenly said, pointing off to the bank of windows. Jodie felt a creeping sensation work its way up her spine as she followed his gesture. She could just make out a woman's face on the other side of the window, dark eyes staring back. Long, greasy hair framed the woman's face, and her tongue was out of her mouth, pressed up against the glazing.

'Oh God,' Jodie uttered, shuddering.

'It's just trying to scare us,' Joe said. 'Probe at our resolve, make us give in to our fear.'

'It's doing a good job,' Jodie replied as the ghostly woman began languidly licking the window.

'Let's go upstairs,' Joe said.

'Can't you force it away with the lantern?'

'We could,' Joe replied. 'But... then what? Just ignore it. Until something is attacking us, we don't need to panic.'

Joe led the way up the stairs, with Jodie constantly looking back over her shoulder as they turned across the half-landing and continued on their way. The hue from the compass started to dull until eventually the glow had dissipated completely.

'See?' Joe said as he eyed the compass as well. 'Nothing to worry about.'

Jodie wasn't convinced. What was more, she was tired of aimlessly wandering, wishing they had something more defined to focus on. While she understood his point about always being on the move—even agreed with it—the idea of just continually walking, stumbling across more of the spirits until eventually being confronted by the dark entity unsettled her.

On top of everything else, she was tired—her legs were aching, and she felt like she had nothing else to give.

Once out of the stairwell, the pair checked inside the sitting room and bedroom in the living quarters. After that, they headed to the corridor and progressed over towards the other wing. Thankfully, with them now being a storey up, Jodie didn't have to worry about something looking back in from outside.

Although... can they fly? she suddenly thought, imagining a spectral entity floating outside, tapping on the window.

As they got closer to the far end of the corridor, her anxiety started to creep up higher. The access to the attic lay just beyond the interconnecting bedroom.

If he suggests going back up there, I'm going to tell him to fuck off, Jodie thought to herself. She'd been up there twice in her life now, and both times she'd had the living daylights scared out of her.

Just as they reached the doorway, Jodie's eyes were again

drawn to the compass. 'Shit, it's glowing again,' she said. The shard stopped spinning and settled in one position, now pointing behind them, the way they'd just come.

Jodie closed her eyes, dreading what she'd see when she turned around. She was forced to open her eyes almost straight away as they both rotated, Joe holding the lantern high.

There was a woman at the end of the hallway, standing with her head cocked to the side.

No, Jodie realised, *not cocked. Her neck has been broken.*

Suddenly, the woman then let out an inhuman roar and burst forward. She moved with savage intent, keeping low, darting towards Jodie and Joe, a snarl on her face. Jodie ducked behind Joe as the man thrust out his lantern. It was enough to force the spectral woman to suddenly stop, turning and lowering her head, narrowing her eyes at the assault of the blue light.

'They're getting braver,' Joe said. 'That's the first time tonight something has tried to attack, rather than just standing and watching.'

Jodie thought about Nathaniel Barrow in the attic. *Not the first time.*

As she stared at the woman, Jodie recognised her as the maid she'd seen earlier alongside the man with the dangling eye. Jodie glanced down at the compass again, wondering where her undead partner was; it was then she noticed something odd about the needle: it kept trying to rotate, fighting to face the opposite direction but then being pulled back. It was as if it was caught between two magnetic pulls.

Then the shard needle snapped to the six o'clock position. Jodie whipped around.

'Joe!' she quickly bellowed.

The man with the dangling eye was dashing towards them, completely silent, moving faster than his strides should have allowed. His arms were outstretched and his one good eye was glaring wildly.

Joe turned the way Jodie had as well, managing to bring the lantern up *just* in time to stop the spirit, though its fingers managed to grasp Jodie around the wrist before the light forced it back. The man's touch was intensely cold. Jodie immediately snatched her hand back. She then glanced back in the other direction to see the woman there starting to advance as well.

'She's coming!' Jodie called in utter panic. Joe looked over his shoulder at her before turning back to the man. He pulled Jodie into the side wall with him, tucking her close, raising the lantern and letting its light wash protectively over them. Its spill allowed both spirits to come relatively close, though they refused to enter where the glow was strongest, simply standing just outside the main illumination.

Adrenaline flooded Jodie's system as she watched the spirits, casting her glance left and right between each one. Her breathing was frantic, teeth clenched, as she pressed herself closer to Joe.

We're trapped.

At this close a distance, she could see more details, noticing just how mottled their skin was. In some areas, the flesh showed signs of heavy decay, with dark meat exposed, sometimes even bone, all bathed in the eerie blue light of the lantern.

While it was clear the woman had been a maid—and evidently maids had not fared well under Barrow's stewardship—she guessed the other ghost had been a handyman of some kind in life. She briefly wondered why Barrow had felt the need to kill him. *Maybe the poor guy stumbled across something he shouldn't have.* Her thoughts were quickly yanked back to the present as the woman tried to shuffle forward, fighting against the light, though she quickly pulled back, wincing once more.

'Shit, shit, shit,' Jodie said. 'What do we do now?'

'We try to keep calm,' Joe said, not exactly sounding it himself. 'Don't panic. They can't get any closer as long as we have the lantern.'

'But... we're stuck here,' she said. 'They're blocking us in.'

I should have just run when I had the opportunity, Jodie thought to herself. *Just taken my chances outside.*

'We'll be okay,' Joe replied. 'Keep close.'

'Why? What are we going to do?'

'We're going to keep moving,' Joe stated.

Jodie's eyes went wide. 'Are you *insane?* Those things are... are... they're *right* there!'

'And we'll force them back,' Joe said. He grabbed her hand. 'Come on, let's move.'

Jodie wanted to resist, wanted to yank the man back towards her as he took his first step, but instead did as instructed, allowing herself to be led while making sure she remained right next to him. The pair moved tentatively towards the maid.

In response, she started to back up, a protective arm still raised across her face.

It's working, Jodie realised. As terrifying as it was to actually be walking *towards* one of the entities, the light was successfully forcing it away. Jodie kept checking back over her shoulder to see the man slowly following, the gaze from his one good eye never leaving them. It reminded Jodie of a tiger in a zoo hungrily watching a park visitor from behind protective glass, leaving the person in no doubt that if the barrier wasn't there, they would be torn limb from limb.

Jodie nervously glanced up at the lantern, focusing her gaze on the flame within, praying that it didn't go out.

'I—I don't know how much more of this I can take,' she whispered, her voice quivering.

'You can take it,' Joe replied firmly. 'Because you have to. Keep going.'

Their progress was painfully slow, the woman before them shuffling back in tandem with every step, the man behind continuing his tentative advance as well.

'Don't you have anything else to use?' Jodie asked in a whisper. 'Any other toys or weapons to get rid of them?'

'No,' Joe replied.

'No rituals or… or something else you can carry out?' Jodie was aware how desperate she sounded and how much she was reaching.

'No,' the man repeated. 'What about you? Anything you can think of?'

'Me?' Jodie asked, surprised. 'What would I know?'

'As I keep saying, you deal with ghosts. How do *you* get rid of them?'

'Well… I'm normally trying to find them, not get rid of them,' Jodie said, still warily watching the retreating woman ahead. 'But… cleansings are supposed to work.'

'Cleansings?'

'Yeah, burning sages and incense, or sprinkling holy water. A lot of people think crystals can be used to clear an area as well. Apparently, they all help remove negative energies. And I've heard salt can be used to form a barrier.'

'Interesting,' Joe said.

'You have any of those things with you?' Jodie asked.

'Unfortunately not,' the man said. 'Though now I'm wishing I did. Next job I'll be sure to bring some.'

Jodie shook her head. As much as Joe had certain things with him that were useful, she still got the sense he was unprepared. She wondered how much training he'd gotten from his enigmatic employers—it didn't sound like very much at all. That only served to unnerve her further, making Jodie think the whole organisation was reckless. She also wondered what the organisation really wanted, what *Joe* really wanted, with the dark spirits. It was clear their intentions were not to free spirits such as the maid or handyman.

Still, regardless of the unpreparedness and lack of experience, Joe was successfully pushing back the spirit ahead, guiding Jodie through the corridor, protected by the light.

Soon, they reached the open door to the connecting bedroom, where the ghostly woman before them shrunk back and entered the room.

'So do we just keep going like this?' Jodie asked. 'Walking around, penned in on either side?'

'I don't know,' Joe admitted. 'I'm thinking on the fly here.'

'If we'd have just stayed in one spot—'

'Then we'd have still gotten surrounded,' Joe snapped. 'Probably even sooner than we did. We wouldn't have been hard to find.'

'I… I guess you're right,' Jodie relented. It occurred to her that blaming Joe wasn't helping their situation. Though she couldn't help but think how if he hadn't shown up in the first place, none of this mess would have ever happened.

With the spirit before them pushed farther back, Jodie and Joe entered the bedroom, Jodie first, with her back tight against Joe's body. She felt his breath on the back of her neck; despite being terrified, the sensation caused a spark of excitement, as insane as that was. That kind of physical closeness to another man, the feeling of being protected merely by his proximity, was something she hadn't experienced in a long time.

She immediately thought of Mark. Shame and guilt swelled up from her gut. The reaction made her want to step forward away from Joe, but fear kept her close.

Once they were in the centre of the bedroom, with the

handyman behind and the maid in front, Jodie heard something: a noise to her side. She turned to her left and saw someone else in the room—a young man pulled himself along the floor, a gaping wound in his neck that showed black meat and a yearning void within the flesh.

'Jesus,' she uttered, once more checking her compass again. The shard was flicking one way, then another, unable to settle. She scolded herself for not looking at it before entering the room, since she'd been so focused on the danger at their front and rear.

'Joe,' she said in a scared whisper.

'I know,' he said, staring at the man on the floor.

Another sound alerted them. Jodie saw a figure stumble forward from the shadows to their right—another woman, this one missing both eyes, which left behind only empty black pits. Her jaw hung at an awkward angle, clearly broken.

Despite the woman not having eyeballs, Jodie noticed the body still couldn't push through the light, turning away just like the others had, which indicated the effect was more than just being blinded by the lantern's light.

It also occurred to Jodie that each spirit harboured brutal injuries of some kind: missing or dangling eyes, broken bones, slashed throats. All indications of violent deaths. Nathaniel Barrow hadn't just killed his victims but had done it messily. She wondered if that was driven merely by anger, or some kind of perversion.

It doesn't matter, she quickly told herself. *Just focus.*

'What do we do?' Jodie asked, feeling overwhelmed.

'Same thing we have been,' Joe said—he sounded surprisingly determined. 'Nothing changes. Two of them or four, it doesn't matter. Just stay under the light and we keep going.'

'Back downstairs?' Jodie asked.

Joe nodded. 'Yeah, back downstairs. Pointless going up to the attic, since there's nowhere to go from there.'

'But then what? What if more show up and just keep us surrounded all night?'

Joe didn't answer.

Suppressing a sigh, Jodie checked the compass again to see it still spinning, struggling to hone in on anything directly. *No surprise there, since we're surrounded.* Up ahead, she spotted a figure standing in the doorway, blocking their progress. It was another maid, wearing the familiar apron, this one torn, as was the dark top she was wearing beneath. The tear there revealed a decayed shoulder with bone visible through rotted flesh. For the first time, Jodie found herself *hoping* the lantern would be strong enough to push them all back, rather than assuming.

It was then she noticed the light from the lantern start to change. The glow had always been constant, with only a slight flicker from the flame. Now, though, it was starting to flicker *wildly,* the flame inside swaying and even jumping. Jodie's heart leapt into her throat. *It's failing! It's going to go out!*

A fresh wave of fear gripped her as Jodie realised she was going to lose the protection of the light. She imagined being completely blinded in the absolute dark while hands reached out and grabbed her. Just like in the attic earlier, only this time she knew the hands wouldn't stop.

I'm going to die.

'It's happening,' Joe said as he gazed up at the lantern. His eyes drifted over and met Jodie's before continuing down to the compass in her hand. She looked down as well.

The shard was glowing, the light emanating from it pulsing as the needle spun manically, faster than she'd seen it, almost a blur. 'The ritual,' Joe went on. 'It's finished. The manifestation is complete.'

Jodie jolted as a deep, inhuman roar sounded from the floor below.

20

'WHAT THE HELL WAS THAT?' SHE ASKED HIM, EYES WIDE. Through the wild flickering of the lantern's light, he could see her body had locked up. 'It came from the hall,' she added.

Joe nodded. 'Yeah, that's where it will manifest: where the initial ritual of provocation took place.' He then pointed to the compass in her hand. The shard inside was slowly pulsing with blue light.

'What's it doing?' she asked with a raised eyebrow.

The needle was firmly pointing beyond the bedroom, now ignoring the other spirits.

'Its dial is drawn to the dark entity,' Joe explained. 'That pulsing is what tells you it's here now, fully realised in our realm.'

Joe took a deep, steadying breath, knowing it was time. He looked around—suddenly, he felt exposed being out in the middle of the room and surrounded on all sides.

'Then why didn't we just wait there for it?' Jodie asked.

'Because I don't want to be near it for what comes next, I

want to buy us as much time as I can. But it'll come to us. I have no doubt of that.'

'So... is it whole now?' Jodie asked. 'The entity. Like, can it just pop up out of anywhere, or is it... I dunno... like a real person, flesh and bone?'

'It can still phase,' Joe replied. 'But briefly. It's in our reality now, so it can't skip back across the veil. But it's also much more powerful, and much angrier. It's going to want to come for us, to take our souls.'

'*What?* Are you fucking kidding me?' Jodie asked, her voice loud.

'Afraid not,' Joe replied. *I know I hinted at it to her before, but I guess she didn't really put that part together.*

He looked over to the side of the room, then took Jodie's arm and started to move her with him. She resisted for a moment. 'Where are we going?' the woman asked.

'Against the wall,' he explained as they both walked between two of the spirits, pushing them back to create enough room for he and Jodie to slip between. Joe led her to the corner, putting the wall to the short hallway behind them. All spirits were now visible in front of them.

No nasty surprises.

Joe held out the lantern to Jodie. 'Take this,' he said, feeling his nerves rise. *Now or never, Joe.* Once Jodie took the light, he lifted her arm up to cast the light farther. 'Keep those things back,' he said.

He squatted down and slipped off his backpack, then started to dig through it. As he did, Joe noticed the spirits around were getting more restless, moving and twitching on the spot; they were clearly desperate to come for him, yet were held back by the light.

'What are you doing?' Jodie asked.

'Getting ready,' Joe replied. He drew out the bundle of

papers and placed them on the floor. Those were the instructions for the rituals, and there were three in total to complete that night. The first, the *Ritual of Provocation,* had already been carried out.

Two to go, then it'll finally be over.

He pulled out the soul vessel and placed that on the ground next to the papers.

'What's that?' Jodie asked. He saw she was looking down.

'Keep an eye on those things,' he replied quickly, not wanting her to inquire further, and Jodie diverted her attention back. Joe glanced up at the spirits as well. They looked like caged animals just waiting to pounce.

'But what *is* it?' Jodie pressed.

'A prison,' he replied.

The soul vessel was an apple-sized crystal orb surrounded by an intricate, wrought-iron lattice around it. The tops and bottoms of the latticework were flattened out, so the tool could stand upright without rolling away.

Lastly, Joe reached into his pocket and took out his folding knife, which he set down as well.

'What the hell do you need *that* for?' Jodie asked, surprise evident.

Joe was reluctant to say anything, but then realised he might need to share more. The girl already knew far too much, but ultimately he knew she would see everything, so what did it matter? *In fact, I might need her help.*

He patted his finger on the pages. 'There are two more rituals to complete here. The first of the two needs to be repeated three times. Then'—he tapped the soul vessel—'I need to spill my blood on this.'

'What? *Why?*' Jodie asked.

'To wake the soul vessel,' Joe said. 'That will bind it to me.'

'Bind it?'

But Joe went on: 'Then there is the last ritual. That again needs to be read three times. But the entity will no doubt be coming for us the whole time.'

'Okay, but what do the rituals *do?*' Jodie asked, glancing down occasionally but keeping her main focus on the nearby spirits that were being kept at bay.

Joe hesitated again. 'The first one I carried out summoned the entity and provoked it. The next one readies the soul vessel. The last one should bind Barrow and imprison him.'

'Just that easy?'

Joe allowed himself a smile. 'I'm not sure how easy it will be, but that's the plan.'

He stood, papers in hand, with the second ritual at the top. He'd repeated it numerous times before coming out that night, but still struggled with the language, the pronunciations completely alien to his untrained tongue—so he'd added the rites spelled out phonetically on each page. Of course, the first ritual had worked, which encouraged him; however much he might mangle his way through it, it seemed to be enough.

Should have had them all memorised, anyway, he told himself. And while that was true, the timing of his mission hadn't really given him the opportunity for that. His hand had been forced.

Joe once again looked out at the dead before him. Seeing them so close, just waiting for their chance to act yet remaining completely silent, was incredibly eerie.

He looked at the pages once more, ready to speak.

Yet before he could, something smashed through the wall behind him, causing Joe to jolt in shock. Jodie cried out as something wrapped around his torso. Joe turned his head and saw that a long arm had punched through the wall just beside him, showering him in debris and gripping him with inhuman strength. It suddenly pulled him back against the plasterboard of the wall so forcefully the surface crumbled and dented inwards.

'Joe!' Jodie screamed.

Joe tried to fight, but his arms were stuck by his sides as the squeezing continued. Through the pain, he kept a tight grip on the papers. He tried to call out to Jodie, who had backed up a step, eyes wide in horror, but he couldn't find the breath.

Joe was pulled again. He felt the wall give way around him as he was yanked right through it. There was a blinding, stabbing pain in his side, both front and back. From experience, he knew something had pierced through him, and in the chaos of being dragged through the wall, he glanced down to see a shaft of broken wood was impaling him on his lefthand side, just above his hip.

He instinctively gripped the papers tighter, desperate not to drop them—they were too important. He had half a mind to try to toss them to Jodie, but had lost sight of her in the falling wall debris. Whatever held Joe suddenly let go, and he fell to the hallway floor, quickly glancing back up again to see the last of the falling debris clearing; a second later, the light of the lantern came through from the newly created hole.

Joe saw a look of sheer terror on Jodie's face. However, she wasn't looking at him, but rather at what was standing above him.

He turned his head farther up to see a decayed hand suddenly reach down for him, the fingers quickly forcing their way into his mouth while a cold palm covered his face. Once it had a firm hold, the hand gripped him and yanked him away. Joe kicked and screamed, but was helpless as he was dragged across the floor, his screams muffled by the hand that held him by the roof of his mouth, thumb pressing into his cheek.

He tasted rotted meat.

Don't drop the rituals! his mind screamed at him, over and over. If he lost them, then both he and Jodie were doomed.

Joe continued to fight as he was pulled towards the attic stairs.

21

Jodie couldn't move.

She was still trying to comprehend what she'd just seen.

Only moments ago, after Joe had explained the plan, she'd felt a surge of hope that things in Parson Hall would soon be at an end. That she would soon be free.

In an instant, Joe had been snatched away.

But it was the thing that'd taken him that had Jodie terrified beyond anything she'd experienced already that night. It was like nothing she'd ever seen before and imbued in her a fear that ran to her very core.

Just like in the attic.

At first, Jodie had only seen a hand burst through the wall, the decayed arm that followed wrapping around Joe. Its flesh was lined with sores and growths, but also rotted away in some areas.

After Joe had been dragged through the wall and the debris had fallen away, Jodie then caught full sight of the thing on the other side—it hadn't been affected by her light in the least.

The entity looked markedly different from the other spirits Jodie had seen that night.

This one was taller, around eight feet in height, and while humanoid, it had been like a twisted recreation. The arms and legs were elongated, as if the limbs had been painfully stretched out.

The skin of the naked entity had been predominantly dark, with welts and small growths dotted around its form, coupled with areas of missing flesh.

Its face, however, had been entirely human, with a bald head and grinning smile—though its mouth had been too wide, which had shown off the stubby teeth.

The eyes… the eyes were what had scared Jodie the most. They bulged, almost popping from the sockets, like the spirit was suffering from a severe case of proptosis. There had been a lining of dark meat around the very edges of the orbs, holding them in place. More disturbingly, the large pupils had been red. So red, in fact, they practically glowed. Even at that distance, Jodie had been able to see the iris was a vertical slit of black, with orangey tendrils running from it and swimming into the surrounding red.

As it had dropped Joe, those eyes had quickly fallen on her and gazed, unblinking. To Jodie, it had felt like she was being studied by something far beyond her comprehension, which had left her feeling tiny and helpless.

She'd also noticed a weird sensation, like something was tapping and probing at her mind, almost like the being had reached out via its gaze and was causing her to enter a frenzy, imparting her with a madness she struggled to contain.

After a few seconds of staring, the dark spirit had reached down, grabbed him by the face, and dragged him out of sight. Jodie had heard his muffled cries, followed by a constant thudding rising up the attic stairs.

Even now, almost a minute later she could barely move, the awful image of Nathaniel Barrow seared into her mind, which was threatening to break. The terror of the experience was so intense, Jodie momentarily forgot the danger still surrounding her.

She hadn't realised her grip on the lantern had grown loose—it was only when it started to slip from her fingers that she suddenly tightened her fist. The movement quickly pulled her back into reality, and she looked around.

The man with the dangling eye was closest to her, but still seemed to respect the lantern's glow and kept his distance. His mouth was pulled into a silent snarl. The others watched her as well, all unblinking, all unmoving, just waiting for their opportunity. Jodie gazed at the lantern, specifically at the wick inside, and she wondered just how long it would burn for.

Not forever, she knew. And once it was finished… then so was she.

Jodie glanced at the pile of rubble on the ground, desperately trying to come up with a plan. She spotted Joe's backpack peeking out beneath a broken length of plasterboard, but she couldn't see the crystal orb he'd been holding.

What had he called it… a soul vessel?

He'd also called it a prison. The idea of it being damaged filled Jodie with dread, knowing if she was to survive, she would need it. The woman slipped the compass into her jacket pocket and knelt down, clearing away the debris with her free hand. In the process, the doubts in her mind sprang up.

Even if you find it, what are you gonna do? Jodie questioned herself. *You don't know what you're doing. Plus, Joe still has the ritual pages.*

Any notions she'd had of finishing things herself quickly drifted away.

After moving more of the rubble away, she soon saw the soul vessel, which she lifted up and examined closely. Other than it being covered in dust, the object appeared fine, with no cracks on the surface of the orb or even bends or dents in the metal. She then pulled the backpack free and checked inside, constantly looking over her shoulder at the spirits to make sure they weren't advancing.

Inside the pack, she found a wrapped blanket and some bundles of cloth. She unfurled one of the bundles and saw an antique-looking mirror with strange markings on the back. *Odd,* she thought. While she had no doubt it was another of Joe's toys and would obviously serve a purpose, she had no idea what that purpose was. With a sigh, she wrapped it again and put it back.

Looking around on the floor some more, she spotted Joe's discarded knife, still folded away, and remembered him saying he had to draw blood into the soul vessel. She then glanced down at her hand, wondering if it had to be his blood specifically, or if her own would do.

Even if yours works, you don't have the rituals, she reminded herself yet again. Even so, she was still thinking of a way to survive, a way to make it through, not quite ready to give up yet. Joe had been right—evidently she had more fight in her than she'd thought.

She had the lantern, but what next? *Do I pack everything up and try to get it to Joe?*

It was certainly an option, though her gut told her the chances of him being okay after being taken were slim.

Which left only one thing: going up to the attic and reclaiming those pages herself. That way, *she* could complete the rituals.

You could run! a voice quickly said. *Go downstairs, get outside, and just go!*

She couldn't deny it was an enticing thought. But as soon as the idea popped into her head, she was reminded again of Joe's warning of what could happen if she went outside.

But you have the lantern, Jodie—just keep forcing them back and escape!

She then looked at the light, wondering if it would indeed be enough to keep her safe outside until she got clear.

A cry of anguish from the attic pulled her from her thoughts. It was Joe. *He's still alive!* Even so, she wondered how long that would be true, given how pained he sounded.

Do I help him?

If she did, that meant going up to the attic.

In fact, completing the rituals herself meant the same thing. Unless he'd dropped the papers somewhere, her path forward was clear.

Stay or go, Jodie, she told herself. *Make a decision.*

And she did. While fleeing was still the more-appealing option, Jodie couldn't shake the notion that Joe was right and she simply wouldn't survive outside. And… there was more to it than that. While she didn't really know the man upstairs, she still couldn't just leave him up there to die. At least not without *trying* to help.

Her mind was made up, though part of her screamed in protest.

Jodie bent down and loaded the soul vessel back into the backpack. She zipped it up, slipped the knife into her pocket, and got back to her feet before slinging the pack over her shoulders.

She glanced again at the spirits that still surrounded her, having no idea how many more were present in the building.

Regardless, she had the lantern; for as long as it burned, she'd have something to keep the threats at bay. She gazed at the wildly flickering light once more.

Please don't go out.

Jodie then slowly moved over to the door and stepped out into the hallway.

22

JOE WAS DEEP IN THE ATTIC, HAVING BEEN THROWN IN AFTER the entity had dragged him up there and closed the door behind them, plunging them both into darkness.

Unfortunately, he'd dropped the rituals when he'd been thrown.

He lay on his back, able to see the sloping roof window thanks to a shaft of moonlight that fell through it. Every breath he took hurt, and when he brought his hand up to his wound, Joe immediately felt the length of wood still poking out of him. The end stuck out around six inches at the front, and after he moved his hand to the back he felt it protrude a few inches there as well. His clothes around the wood were wet, making his hands slick with blood—a lot of blood.

Shit.

He wondered if he should try to pull the length of wood out—his army training told him he shouldn't, since it would be like pulling a stopper out, causing him to lose even more blood.

'I'm... watching,' an inhuman voice said from somewhere

in the dark. Joe's heart seized. The voice sounded... demonic. Scratchy, pained, and somehow ancient. *'Always... watching.'*

Joe turned his head in the direction of the voice, which was deeper in the room, and gasped—pain shot through his torso at the breath. He could only see one thing of the entity.

Its eyes.

Two red orbs hung in the darkness, wild and penetrating in their unblinking gaze, standing out against the utter darkness around them.

'No,' Joe uttered—for the first time that night, panic overtook him. He tried to scramble away, but the pain in his side was too intense, and when he tried to roll to his front, he almost vomited at the explosion of agony.

Joe nearly wanted to avert his gaze, but felt compelled to stare back at those eyes. His body suddenly locked up as the orbs started to draw closer.

'No!' he cried out again. Joe couldn't explain why, but merely being watched by them was striking him with an unnatural terror. Sure, the situation was scary, but he'd already seen a *lot* that night, and none of it had affected him this much. So he couldn't understand why his mind was now threatening to break.

There was no sway as the eyes continued their advance, no indication that the hidden entity was walking as a normal person would. Instead, the eyes seemed to just drift in complete silence.

More terror gripped Joe, enough for him to fight through the pain and start to crawl away, trying his best to keep from throwing up with every movement. The wood poking from his front scraped across the floor as he crawled on his stomach, since he was unable to push himself up on all fours. Eventually, he couldn't hold back anymore and purged, throwing up what had been bubbling in his gut. He tasted copper in his mouth and knew at least some of what he'd expelled was blood.

Not good.

But it was hard to worry too much about internal bleeding at that moment—it was hard to think about *anything* except those maddening eyes that continued to drift closer. Soon, they loomed over him, looking down. Joe heard a deep, animalistic sound, something approaching a chuckle, but… off.

'S-stay back,' Joe cried in desperation. He wanted to turn away yet still couldn't avert his eyes.

A throbbing pain pulsed through his head, like a chisel was tapping away at his brain, threatening to crack his mind and shatter it into a thousand pieces.

The eyes above him drew nearer still as the thing bent down.

'Get away!' Joe yelled.

He felt the entity take hold of the wood that stuck out of him. The spirit then yanked, dislodging the shaft in one quick pull—Joe screamed in pain. He felt liquid spill freely from the open wound left behind.

There was another demonic chuckle. A large, cold hand found his wound and pushed its long fingers inside.

Joe continued to scream.

23

JODIE HESITATED IN THE SHORT HALLWAY AT THE SOUND OF THE awful cries of pain echoing down through the stairwell.

What's it doing to him?

Her decision to go up to help Joe now seemed foolish, her resolve close to breaking. The ghosts behind her had huddled around the doorway to the bedroom, clustered together and waiting for the light to move away enough for them to follow. Their forms flickered in the blue light as they silently watched.

Keep going! You need those pages.

While Jodie knew that was true, it still didn't make her next step any easier. She eyed the door to the stairwell warily, where cries of pain continued to drift down.

She looked at the lantern. Given it seemed to repel the other spirits, Jodie wondered if she could simply bolt up the stairs to the attic, drive Nathaniel Barrow back, and help Joe. But she quickly remembered the first sight she'd had of the entity's full form—it had been bathed in the light of the lantern then and hadn't so much as flinched. *Maybe because it was farther away?* she considered, hoping the lantern would be more effective up close. Regardless, Jodie knew she needed to act, and she finally found the strength to take a step forward.

Thump.

Jodie suddenly paused at hearing the heavy footstep on the stairs.

Thump.

Jesus Christ, what now?

Thump.

Jodie held the lantern out before her, over towards the door, waiting for another footstep—which didn't come. Whatever was on the stairs clearly didn't want to enter into the light. She wondered if it was Nathaniel, and the thought of seeing those red eyes again filled her with dread. She held her arm out farther, moving the lantern away from her and forcing more light into the staircase, even leaning forward to give herself more reach.

Yet despite that, she still couldn't see anything on the stairs. Jodie was about to inch forward when something grabbed hold of her ankle.

Jodie whipped her head down in shock to see two hands and instantly realised what had happened. She'd pushed the lantern so far away from herself her body had cast an area behind her in shadow. One of the ghosts was on the floor and it gripped her lower left leg with both hands, staring up at her with dead, unblinking eyes.

No!

Jodie didn't have time to turn with the light before she was yanked backwards with such ferocity the lantern fell from her grasp; it clattered to the floor and rolled away from her. Jodie's heart was in her mouth, worried the glass would shatter or the flame would extinguish.

Though the lantern remained intact and alight, she was

pulled farther backwards—she clawed desperately trying to reach the lantern.

Which remained agonisingly out of reach.

Jodie turned her head and stared in horror at the decomposing maid that held her. She kicked out and fought against the grip. In response, the ghoul's hold shifted—for a moment, Jodie thought she was free. But the maid's hands quickly found Jodie's boot and pulled once again.

Other spirits started to crawl forward, moving over the maid, each seeming like a zombie desperate for its next meal. Jodie screamed and tried to kick out, but couldn't move her leg. She brought her other foot up and thrust that forward instead. The sole of her boot connected with the woman's face and snapped the woman's head back, but the spectre's expression didn't change, not even registering the kick.

The other entities slithered ever closer, Jodie's old friend the handyman with the dangling eye front and centre.

I'm going to die.

She knew in just a few moments the hanging-eyed man and the others would reach her and she'd be drowned under the undead mob.

She screamed and fought, utterly desperate.

Utterly terrified.

Then… she felt something. Jodie's foot shifted in her boot as the maid pulled at her leg, and the more Jodie pulled, the more her foot started to come free. Jodie yanked her foot repeatedly, inching it out farther and farther each time.

Come on!

The maid held on with her iron grip, and the handyman crawled closer, reaching out towards Jodie's other leg.

Come on!

Finally, Jodie's foot slipped completely free. She quickly yanked both legs back just as the handyman's fingers scraped against her shin. Jodie spun and scrambled over to the lantern, grabbing it and turning back in an instant, holding it out before her, teeth clenched in both fear and anger. Now under the wash of the blue light, the entities in the doorway instantly recoiled, faces all locked in snarls as they fought their way back through the doorway, turning their heads away from the lantern with grimaces of pain.

'Get the fuck back!' she seethed, pushing the lantern out farther, taking joy in how pained the spirits seemed to be. Soon enough, they'd all managed to untangle themselves and had retreated into the bedroom, where they hid away from the light.

Jodie allowed herself a few moments for her frantic heartrate to drop. The arm that held the lantern shook and her teeth chattered, adrenaline flooding her and mixing with the anger and fear in an unwelcome cocktail that was hard for her to control. Eventually, her eyes fell on her discarded boot. The entities were far back enough for her to retrieve it safely now, so she tentatively set the lantern down next to her, then slid the boot back on and tied the laces. Her fingers trembled so much it took her three attempts.

Once done, Jodie retrieved the lantern and got back to her feet, legs unsteady. On the verge of tears, she forced herself to walk again, moving to the stairs—but not the stairs to the attic. She carried on to the flight that would take her down to the entrance.

She was done.

As awful as she felt leaving Joe behind, she no longer had it in her to help him. All she wanted to do was to get outside and run, hoping the lantern would be enough to keep her safe. Once clear, she would find a way to call the police and get someone else out here to help.

Get someone else out here to die, a voice said in her mind. She tried to ignore it, though. This wasn't her mess—and it wasn't her responsibility.

The hell with all of it!

Once at the top of the stairs, she looked down into the yawning dark, then glanced back over her shoulder to see those damn spirits inching out of the doorway again. *They don't give up.*

She was about to take her first step when she heard something behind her again.

Thump.

More footsteps on the attic stairs.

Thump. Thump.

After turning around to check, Jodie saw a hand grip the doorframe; a large man leaned out, his face bloated and grey, clearly the entity she'd heard before when wondering if it was Barrow.

Jodie ignored it and looked forward again. She'd taken only a single step as another cry of pain came from above. Jodie didn't know Joe well, but didn't doubt he was tough, so she shuddered at what could make him scream like that.

Best not find out for yourself. She took another step. He screamed again.

A pang of guilt stopped Jodie. *You're the only one that can help him. You know that.*

She tried to fight against it, reasoning that even if she went up, there would be nothing she could do. Only die alongside him.

Jodie took another step. And another. Joe's cries continued, the pain of them—the utter agony—cutting to Jodie's core.

After pausing, she started to cry, knowing she was leaving him to an awful death. *Go. You can't help him.* She took another step, still wrestling with herself, tears flowing freely, guilt building and building.

Another step. And another. *That's it. Keep going.*

But… she couldn't.

She was unable to move anymore. Her body simply wouldn't react, the guilt just too much. So… she just stood on the steps, listening to Joe's distant wails.

I can't abandon him, she realised, despite what her survival instincts were telling her. The sounds of his agony were too much to ignore. They'd haunt her nightmares forever.

Joe had told her earlier she was capable of more than she knew. As she turned around, she dearly hoped he was right.

You'll die if you go up there, she told herself, the part of her that wanted to flee trying to reason with her one final time.

But Jodie didn't listen. She started to climb the stairs once more.

24

Joe's voice was hoarse from crying out, his throat scratched and raw like his gullet was lined with shards of glass.

But as painful as it was, his ragged voice barely registered. He was too focused on the searing agony in his side, too focused on trying to keep his mind from breaking as the maddening red eyes glared down at him, penetrating his mind.

Joe was being held by the throat in a vice-like grip, easily keeping him in place no matter how much Joe fought. The unseen entity seemed to take joy in alternating its grip strength, periodically squeezing his neck tight enough to cut off his breath and make Joe fight for air before loosening it a moment later.

But it was the hand that rummaged around in his side that drew most of Joe's focus. The agony it brought was excruciating.

He felt cold fingers probe and explore, pressing against his intestines, gripping and pinching at them, even tearing them.

Finally, the hand pulled free with a *squelch*. Joe coughed out a spray of blood. He thought of Gemma, knowing he'd failed her.

Again.

25

ONE YEAR AGO...

Joe looked down at her. His chest felt tight.

Gemma coughed over and over, struggling for breath.

She's a husk, he realised. All her former vibrance and mischievous energy had been replaced by a withered, pale version of the woman he loved.

'You okay?' he asked once Gemma had managed to regain control.

She took a slow breath and nodded. Her pale eyes found him as she looked up from her position in the bed. A sad smile spread over her lips. 'Do I look that bad?' she asked.

'What do you mean?' Joe replied.

She laughed. The sound was weak. 'Your face... you look horrified. Have I faded away that much in a week?'

Her words stung. The way she'd said 'week' felt like a barb.

But then... so what? She was right. That was how long it had been since Joe was last at the hospice. She was the one person in this world that he truly loved, yet he could barely bring himself to see her when she needed him most.

'You look fine,' he said, not sure what else to offer. He let his eyes wander, not able to meet hers any longer, and studied the drip she was hooked up to that administered pain relief. Judging by her near-constant winces of discomfort, Gemma didn't seem to be getting much relief at all. The room smelled like antiseptic and had a cold, sterile feel that Joe hated.

Six months, he said to himself. That was how long it had taken for his life to fall apart. In actuality, after the initial diagnosis, Gemma had only been given three months to live *at best*.

She'd doubled that. Because she was a fighter. Just like Joe was.

No, like you thought *you were. You fucking coward.*

With every month that had passed, Joe had pulled back more and more. As weak of him as it was, he just couldn't cope with what he was seeing and how rapidly she was degrading before his eyes. It was too much.

He loved her. Truly loved her. She was the only person he'd ever felt that way about. Yet seeing what the disease was doing to her was simply more than he could bear.

Joe had watched people he'd known die before. He'd seen them shot, stabbed, some even blown up right before his eyes. In every instance, he'd managed to compartmentalise it, tuck any emotion away and carry on. The soldiers he'd seen die were his colleagues, his brothers in arms, but there had still been a distance there. He'd never let anyone get too close.

Dealing with death had just been part of his job. Something to accept and get on with.

This was different. It was Gemma.

She was the only person he'd ever let get close. The one he wanted to spend all his waking hours with, and the woman who had given him purpose after leaving the military.

And now she was fading away.

Coming to see her was a monumental effort for Joe, because every second in her company was a fight not to break down. Once he was back in his car alone, the flood-gates always opened, and it took days for them to close again enough for him to operate in everyday life.

He felt guilt, of course, and a constant voice nagged him to go back there—Gemma needed him. But he'd always fought against it, finding it all too painful.

'I've—I've missed you,' Gemma suddenly said, her voice cracking. Joe turned his eyes to her. He saw tears running down her face.

'What do you mean?' he asked, taken off guard. 'I'm right here.'

She shook her head. 'You're not, Joe.' More tears came. 'You're hiding from me. Keeping away. *Running*. Am I… am I that repulsive to you?'

'What?' Joe said, leaning down closer to her. He placed a hand on hers. 'No, of course not. Why would you say that?'

'Because I never see you,' she said, crying. 'And I need you. I have no one else.' She tried to squeeze his hand affectionately, but the weak grip he felt showed just how frail she was.

'You do see me,' Joe argued defensively, even though he knew she was right. He just didn't like that she was vocalising it, holding up a mirror for him to see his own shameful reflection. 'I come by all the time,' he went on. She frowned, giving him a tearful *don't lie to me* stare. She didn't say anything and just let his words hang over them, waiting for him to continue. 'I do,' he went on, again entirely too defensive—like he was trying to convince himself. Gemma still said nothing, just stared, more tears streaming down her gaunt cheeks. Seeing her like that made Joe's dam break. His own tears started to flow. He desperately tried to hold them back, trying to shut off the overwhelming emotion. Doing so was instinctual for him.

'It's okay, baby,' Gemma said, her fingers trying again to squeeze his hand.

'It's not!' Joe snapped and straightened up, pulling his hand back and causing Gemma's eyes to widen with shock. '*None* of this is okay!' Joe felt his chest tighten even more. The room seemed smaller, like it was closing in on all sides, ready to crush him. He started to hyperventilate.

I... I need to get out of here. He backed up.

'Calm down, Joe,' Gemma said to him, reaching a hand up, almost begging him to come back to her. 'It's okay, just... calm down.'

'Stop saying it's okay,' Joe said through gritted teeth. 'It's not. It's *not*. I can't... I can't...'

He looked over to the door desperately, the urge to run overwhelming.

'No, Joe,' Gemma said. 'Please.' He glanced over to her to see she was shaking her head, knowing what he was planning. She looked so sad, so scared. It broke his heart, yet also just served to make the room feel smaller still, make his chest feel tighter. He couldn't catch his breath. He looked to the door again.

'I... I'm sorry,' he said, continuing to sob. 'I'm so... s-sorry.' Joe couldn't look at her, knowing what he was about to do. 'I just can't...'

He didn't finish and ran towards the door.

'Joe, no!' Gemma called, her voice weak but desperate. 'Please!'

That one word—*please*—was enough to stop him in his tracks. *What are you doing? You can't leave her like this!*

Even so, Joe couldn't bring himself to turn around and look back. He couldn't stomach seeing what the disease had done to her, how much it had stripped her of all that she used to be.

You're weak, he chastised himself. *Not worthy of her. You never were.*

Joe took off running, fleeing the hospital and leaving Gemma's desperate calls behind.

After that, he didn't return to the hospice. Gemma died two weeks later. Despite his guilt, Joe couldn't even bring himself to attend the funeral.

For the following six months, he lived a miserable life, with thoughts of ending it all a constant presence. *Maybe then I can see her again and apologise for what I did,* he thought to himself regularly.

But deep down, he knew seeing her again was just a fantasy. There was no afterlife, nor any chance at redemption. Gemma was dead now, not existing anywhere.

On top of that, there was no one to apologise to. No one to offer forgiveness.

Eventually, Joe forced himself to visit Gemma's grave. Gemma had had no one else in life, so her funeral had been a basic, council-arranged affair. Because of that, the headstone at the cemetery was a simple, rectangular block of granite with her name engraved on it. There were no flowers on the grave when Joe arrived—not even dead ones to show someone had stopped by.

Jesus. I'm so sorry, Gemma. You deserved better.

Standing before her headstone, he bent down and set the flowers he'd bought into the plastic pot fixed to the base. After spending a few moments trying to make sure they were nicely displayed, he stood back up and looked around. As far as he could tell, he was the only one in the area. While it wasn't particularly cold, the first hint of rain was starting to fall, lightly coating his face, but not strong enough to be an annoyance.

Joe waited, just staring at the grave, at the flowers, feeling uncomfortable and not sure what he was supposed to say. He clasped his hands in front of his midsection, something he'd seen people do when trying to be respectful. After a moment he opened his mouth to speak to the grave, something else he'd heard people did at cemeteries… but no words came out. *What's the point? She's dead and gone.*

After being there for less than two minutes, Joe decided it was time to go.

Running again, little coward?

He turned and took a few steps. As he did, a light breeze blew over him. Then… something made him turn around, something he couldn't explain. A feeling.

When he did, he frowned in confusion.

The flowers were on the floor.

The pot hadn't tipped over, and the breeze hadn't been strong enough to blow the flowers out of the container.

For a moment, it was almost as if Gemma herself was rejecting his gesture. But he shook his head. *That's impossible.*

Giving it no more thought, Joe turned and left, not stopping this time on his way back to the gate. Only when he was there did he look back.

He paused again. Not only paused, but gasped. There was a woman in white standing near the grave.

Gemma?

Joe's mouth went dry as he stood in stunned silence, unable to accept what he was seeing. Though the woman was a good distance away, he was sure it was her.

Certain.

Am I hallucinating? He quickly brought his hands up and rubbed his face. When he lowered them… the woman was gone. *It… can't be.*

The event played over and over in Joe's mind over the coming days.

Then, the following week, he was woken up in the middle of the night by something violently shaking his leg. When Joe sat up in panic, he found the room empty. However, after flicking on his nightlight, he soon saw the photo of Gemma he kept on the bedside table was now on the floor, frame and glass smashed as if it had been stomped on.

Following that, more activity occurred, with Joe constantly up during the night, or returning home to find things trashed. Once he even saw something slide off his kitchen counter with no way to explain how. Though he was hesitant at first, he soon accepted that Gemma was not quite done with him. He so desperately wanted to see her, to talk to her, to just tell her how sorry he was. Yet no matter how much he shouted those words to the open air, it didn't change anything. Didn't quell her anger.

If I could just see her, face her somehow, and tell her I regret what I did... She'd listen, I know she would.

It wasn't until a chance encounter with a man in a bar months later presented him with the opportunity to do just that.

26

MORE PAIN. JOE SCREAMED. THE HAND FOUND HIS WOUND YET again and fingers tore once more at the edges. Those eyes still drilled into his own. The realisation that Joe was going to die soon shook him.

He'd never been terrified of death—he'd run headlong into too many dangerous situations for that—but he *was* terrified of what death at Parson Hall meant.

Joe had often thought if he died, he might be able to see Gemma again and give her the apology she deserved. But if he died here, there would be no opportunity to see his beloved again; instead, he'd be trapped there, just another puppet for the dark spirit to control.

An eternal torment in death.

Joe coughed blood again.

'Please,' he managed to wheeze up. It was futile, but he was desperate. 'Please… don't.'

In response, he heard that inhuman chuckle return. The hand wormed its way farther into his insides.

27

'GET BACK!' JODIE SNARLED AT THE BLOATED ENTITY ON THE stairs ahead of her. He had on dirty fabric trousers but no top, exposing a rotund belly that had a gash across its middle. Dark intestines poked out of the wound.

The man was driven back by the lantern, forced up the stairs as Jodie advanced. She kept the lantern close to her body this time and had pressed herself against the side wall to ensure the light traveling back down behind wasn't blocked by her body.

She wouldn't make the same mistake again.

The spirits from below had followed her, as expected, cramming en masse into the stairwell at the bottom, just at the edge of the light, which bathed them in its eerie, flickering glow.

A fresh howl of agony came from the attic above her. While Jodie had no idea what was happening to Joe, she figured that if the dark spirit *was* killing him, it was sure taking its time.

Which meant it was likely revelling in the torture it was inflicting. Jodie briefly wondered if that sadism was from

Nathaniel himself, or born from the festering dark spirit that had merged with him.

Probably both, she reasoned.

Part of her wanted to scream up to Joe, to tell him she was coming, to just hold on a little longer. She didn't, of course, not wanting to broadcast her approach to the entity.

Jodie continued up, forcing the bloated, semi-naked man out into the vestibule. She kept going and eventually the man was pressed back against the cross wall that separated the vestibule from the attic itself. He bumped against it and stopped, as did Jodie, suddenly curious what would happen to him now that he had nowhere else to go and no way to escape the light.

Jodie glanced behind to the stairwell again and saw the head of a maid rise into view, then stop, unwilling to come forward any farther. Resolve steeled, Jodie took a step forward, washing the rotund man in more of the lantern's light. He turned his head to the side, clamped his eyes shut, and shrieked while also pushing against the wall, desperate to get through.

It's hurting him, Jodie realised. She pressed forward, feeling a surge of vengeful glee overtake her at its obvious pain. *Take that, you fucker.*

But as Jodie continued closer, the entity suddenly forced itself *through* the wall, leaning into its structure so much the plasterboard bent and buckled, giving way. The spirit then fully broke through and retreated into the dark space beyond as loose plasterboard and dust particles fell to the floor. The moment the wall opened up, Joe's wails of pain became clearer.

Jodie was shocked. She wasn't sure what she'd expected to happen, but it certainly wasn't to see the spirit literally destroy a wall just to get away. Still, as she stared into the hole, she realised it might not have been such a bad thing.

Last time she had been in the attic, an unknown force had held the door shut, preventing her escape.

Now that would no longer be an issue—she had a ready-made escape route. Not hesitating anymore, Jodie moved towards the door and placed a tentative hand on the handle. As expected, it didn't budge.

She then moved sideways to the hole in the wall, holding her light up to it... but she couldn't bring herself to step any closer, knowing what was waiting inside.

If you're going to go... just go.

Yet that was easier said than done. Because once inside, she would be in the presence of Nathaniel Barrow once more. She remembered seeing his eyes in there before, the red then dull and appearing only briefly—most likely because he hadn't completed his manifestation yet. She also remembered how the dark spirit had assaulted her and she shivered at the memory.

Keep going! she ordered herself again.

Jodie forced herself closer to the hole, still hearing Joe, though he wasn't crying out anymore—the sounds had changed to a sob. Jodie peered inside the attic space, keeping the lantern close to her, and saw the space directly in front of the hole; there were exposed, dusty floorboards, but nothing else.

After taking a breath to steel herself, Jodie gritted her teeth and moved through, sliding sideways to avoid the broken timber studs that jutted out at awkward angles.

She felt her coat snag briefly, but was still able to force herself through, and once on the other side she held up the lantern to illuminate more of the attic.

She saw Joe deeper in the space, lying on the floor, just on the edge of her light, groaning and slowly writhing in obvious pain. There was a smattering of blood on his face and the man clutched at his side.

Jodie could also see the large ghost that had forced his way through the wall. He was still retreating from her, crouched low and scampering backwards with surprising speed and agility, eventually disappearing into the shadows.

While she couldn't see the dark spirit's form she *could* see its damn eyes, hovering beyond Joe, its body lost to the darkness. The eyes stood in stark contrast to the black around them.

The entity's gaze was focused entirely on Jodie.

She froze, more fear and panic flooding her body, rising and rising and threatening to bubble over.

On the floor, Joe slowly turned his head and his eyes fell on Jodie. A look of surprise washed over him, briefly replacing his pained expression. She wanted to call out to him, to beg him to crawl over to her, yet she couldn't find her voice. She watched as his gaze left her and drifted across the floor, looking at something. Jodie followed his gaze and saw them.

The papers.

They lay in a cluster midway between Joe and Jodie, just over to her right.

'Get them,' Joe said. 'Quickly and go.' He coughed again—which released a spurt of blood. 'Do the first ritual, then… draw your blood on the…' He devolved into a coughing fit.

'I—I know,' Jodie said, voice shaking. She remembered what he'd said: first ritual three times, spill blood on the soul vessel, then the second ritual three times.

'G—go,' Joe forced out, his gaze desperate. Jodie glanced up at the red eyes that continued to stare at her. Another wave of terror washed over her—and not just terror, but madness. She felt a stabbing pain inside her head, as if a needle was sliding directly into her brain.

She couldn't understand what was happening, nor how the mere gaze of the entity was enough to provoke such a physical reaction in her. Jodie quickly forced herself to look away, her eyes settling on the papers once more. Even so, she could still feel something tapping away inside her skull, chipping away at her sanity.

Focus, Jodie told herself, trying to break through the mental barrier that had rooted her to the spot. The ritual papers couldn't have been more than ten feet away. *Just run over and grab them, then get the hell out of the attic.*

She had no idea where she would go once she'd retrieved them, but she knew she couldn't do what she needed to in the attic. Not with that thing so close.

'Go,' Joe said again, triggering yet another coughing fit. Every breath he sucked in sounded wet and wheezy.

Jodie didn't give herself another second to think, knowing any further delay would just lead to her talking herself out of acting.

Instead, she bolted, heading straight over to the scattered papers. She quickly gathered them together with her free hand, grasping them tightly as she stood. Her focus then turned back to Joe, as well as the red eyes behind him.

Only, the eyes weren't behind Joe anymore. And Nathaniel Barrow was no longer lost to the shadows.

Jodie couldn't help but let out a shriek. The demonic entity now standing *in front* of Joe, fully revealed by the blue light—and clearly unaffected by it.

Jodie sprinted away in fright, though the dark spirit wasn't moving, simply standing motionless, long arms down by its side. Its visage was repulsive, the body dotted with welts, sores, and bumpy growths, and Jodie couldn't help glancing down at where its genitals should have been, where there was only a sore-lined mound.

A slow smile then crept across the entity's mouth, which displayed its stubby teeth. It casually tilted its head to the side.

'I've... been... watching,' it said. A creeping sensation worked its way up Jodie's spine at hearing the utterly inhuman voice. *'And* she... *is... watching you.'*

Jodie paused. *She* was watching? Her mind was immediately drawn back to the Manor House a few nights ago and what the little boy had said to her.

'She's noticed you.'

Even in her state of panic, Jodie couldn't help but draw the similarities; her gut told her they were both talking about the same person.

However, Jodie had no idea who this 'she' was, nor did she have any clue what it all meant.

'W… who?' Jodie managed to choke out. '*Who* is watching me?'

The entity said nothing and instead ran a fat, black tongue over its teeth, head still tilted to one side.

'Jodie,' Joe wheezed from the floor. 'Please… just… go.'

Heeding his plea, Jodie ran, heading straight over to the hole in the wall, lantern waving wildly as she moved. She clutched the papers tightly, feeling them crinkle and fold in her grasp.

As she ducked through the gap towards the vestibule, her coat snagged yet again, jolting her to a stop.

Shit!

She turned and looked back. The dark spirit was closer now. It was still standing motionless, though it had somehow covered a few feet in a blink.

'Come on!' she cried out in desperation as she yanked at her coat, trying to untangle herself using the hand that also held the papers.

Shit, shit, shit!

Eventually, she managed to free her jacket and practically fell through the opening out into the vestibule.

After regaining her footing, Jodie continued on towards

the stairs, sprinting over to see the ghouls that had previously been following her were still there—one visible at the head and others packed in behind the leader. Jodie just held her lantern high and roared in anger. She knew the light would make them retreat, but she had no time for that to happen slowly. While running, Jodie allowed herself a brief glimpse behind, where she saw Nathaniel Barrow on the other side of the hole, leaning down to gaze out at her.

The entity was still smiling.

That spurred Jodie on, so she sprinted to the stairs; the spirits there filtered down quickly, the ones at the head pushing back into those below them, wincing and snarling, hands held aloft to ward off the light.

She thundered towards them as the pained cries of the spirits rose in intensity, the ones at the front unable to retreat quickly enough to escape the glow. But Jodie had no intention of slowing down, feeling a surge of glee at the pain she was causing them.

Several steps later, Jodie caught herself, remembering the spirits were just puppets, trapped in the gravity of the dark entity and twisted by it, controlled by it, their actions not their own.

She wondered if the pure part of their souls still existed in there somewhere, watching what was happening, feeling the pain from the lantern.

It cut her glee short, though didn't slow her down. Regardless of everything, she still had to get away.

As she progressed down the stairs, Jodie's mind tried to settle on just *where* she would run to. She wanted to put as much distance as she could between her and Barrow, to give herself time to work. Her mind ran to the old hall. While one location would be just as good as another, the lure of the open window in that space appealed to her, offering a possible escape route should things not go well.

The ghosts finally emptied out at the bottom of the stairs, falling like bowling pins. Jodie rushed out after them into the hallway. She again glanced at the wildly flickering flame, trying to focus on the wick to see how much time she had left, but it was difficult to make much out with her frantic movement.

Jodie quickly turned and rushed over to the next stairwell, with the entities around her all pressing themselves into the wall, desperate to get away but completely trapped. Their moans and groans reached the intensity of a scream, reminding Jodie of the weak sounds a deathly ill person might make as they suffered.

She had no idea if there were any other ghosts in the building besides the ones she'd just traveled through. After all, Nathaniel Barrow's true body count had never been determined.

Please let that be all.

Jodie dashed through the doorway and moved down the stairs, glancing back up when at the half-landing to see if Barrow was following. She couldn't see him, but some of the other spirits had gathered at the top.

Don't follow, damn it!

Their relentlessness was horrifying.

Realising she could do nothing about it, Jodie kept her focus on the way ahead as she ran, eventually coming out into the function room.

Because the space there was large, she briefly considered pausing so she could start with the first ritual, but kept going; she wanted to get as far away as possible, still thinking of the open window.

While running, a thought suddenly struck her, forcing Jodie to glance down at the papers in her hand.

I don't know which one is first!

She looked at the top page, slowing just a hair so she

could make out what was printed, hoping there was some kind of clue to indicate what she should start with.

Though it was difficult to read while moving, she saw there were a few different sections on the top sheet, with some things written in English but most in an unknown language. At the top, there was a title: *Ritual of Imprisonment (Kara'meth An'dural - imprisoning the spirit).*

That's the final one, she realised. *Gotta be!* As Jodie scanned the page, she saw what she assumed to be the rite typed out first in the foreign language, and then it was written out again phonetically. Last was an English translation, but she was still jogging too quickly to take in the details.

Soon enough, Jodie found herself in the old hall, which was thankfully empty. She ran to the far end, close to the window, and stopped, gasping in a few breaths as she turned back to face the door. She then slipped off the backpack and knelt down, setting the bag and lantern close to each other.

Jodie kept glancing ahead as she took everything out of the pack, first unfurling the large blanket and setting it on the floor to give her a place to work, then moving the lamp so it was on the blanket as well. The stones she'd seen Joe use earlier that night had been wrapped inside the material, so she kept them to one side, all piled together, hoping she wouldn't need them. Each oval stone had a flat top, but now that she was close to them, she could see that each had a strange marking carved into that flat surface as well.

Runes? she wondered, but didn't allow herself to dwell on them any longer. Joe hadn't mentioned them being part of the remaining rituals, so she figured it wouldn't be an issue to ignore them.

Next, she retrieved the shard compass from her pocket and set it down next to the lamp, the shard needle inside still pulsing, facing directly at the door. Jodie dug out Joe's knife, unfolded the long blade, and finally retrieved the soul vessel.

After that, she thumbed through the sheets of paper, seeing some pages were just more layouts of the building, like the ones she'd seen outside. Three of the sheets contained rites, however, so she separated those out and put the rest down.

While the *Ritual of Imprisonment* was at the top, she also saw the *Ritual of Provocation,* which she assumed to be the one Joe had read aloud earlier that night. Finally, there was one simply titled *The Opening of the Vessel.*

Bingo!

She wondered if these sheets had been given to Joe as instructions, or if he had prepared them himself, given their basic formatting and the thin, low-quality paper.

Movement suddenly drew her attention and her gaze lifted to a window on the opposite side of the room. There, she jolted at the sight of a shadowy figure peeking inside at her, face pressed up against the glass.

Jesus Christ!

The window was far enough away that the light from the lantern didn't fully illuminate it, so she couldn't really make out the person, but she felt unnerved being under its watchful gaze all the same.

Ignore it and carry on, she told herself, sure more of the spirits would likely show up soon anyway.

It was when Nathaniel Barrow made an appearance that she'd really have to worry.

Jodie quickly brought the rite she needed to the top and scanned it, trying to determine just what language it was written in.

What does it matter? You can't read it, so just speak it.

While she would have been worried about mangling the pronunciation, the section that phonetically spelled out the rites was a godsend; she was grateful that Joe—or whoever had completed the documents—had been so thorough. Jodie happened to glance up. She froze.

The handyman was back, standing in the doorway, loose eye still dangling at his cheek by a length of fleshy optic nerve. She saw other spirits shift and move behind him.

Ignore them.

Jodie took a breath and focused on the words, scanning through the page:

The Opening of the Vessel (Rasu'an Nika'theh).

Aru-ka nemi talan oshira,

Esho'nai vatu menah.

Soru-ka deni tamah-ya,

Uraka shen toh no varu

The section after that showed the same rite spelled phonetically.

Aru-ka NEM-ee TAH-lahn oh-SHEE-rah

EH-shoh-nigh VAH-too MEH-nah

SOH-roo-kah DEH-nee TAH-mah-yah

OO-rah-kah shen toh noh VAH-roo

Lastly was the English translation:

Open the mouth of the hollow gate,

Let the vessel know its hunger.

Wake the shell that drinks the soul,

Bind the fleshless one to the wound.

While it sounded like gibberish to her, Jodie focused on the phonetic verse and began to speak: 'Aru-ka nemi talan oshira,' she said, slowly and deliberately. *Please be right,* she silently prayed after that first line, hoping she hadn't butchered the words. Then she went on: 'Esho'nai vatu menah.'

A sudden smack on one of the windows—hard enough to crack the glass—caused her to jump. Jodie whipped her head around and saw a hand outside strike one of the windows a second time. He punched it again and again, a spiderweb of cracks spreading out. The entities in the doorway ahead began to moan and wail, their voices growing louder. Jodie focused on the page and again kept going. 'Soru-ka deni tamah-ya. Uraka shen toh no varu.'

One repetition done.

The cries rose higher, increasing in pitch, becoming squeals that were hard to listen to—it was a struggle for Jodie not to clamp her hands over her ears. The hand that slapped the glass continued to beat at it and the window soon shattered, with broken shards flying inwards.

'Aru-ka nemi talan oshira,' Jodie said, starting her second go round, realising everything happening around her was all just a distraction. 'Esho'nai vatu menah.'

She then completed her second reading of the rite and immediately started on the third, going through it as quickly as she could while still keeping her words clear. Once she'd finally finished, she looked down at the soul vessel on the blanket, which had drawn her attention. She saw a faint blue light spark in the centre of the orb.

It worked!

Her jubilation was short-lived as Jodie realised she would now need to cut herself. She pushed through her trepidation and knelt down, retrieving the knife. Another of the windows exploded inwards before she could do anything else, causing her to instinctively duck. The squeals of the dead rose even higher in intensity. Fortunately, the lantern continued to hold everything back.

Jodie didn't allow herself to think about what she was going to do and simply acted, slicing the sharp edge of the blade across her palm. An immense searing pain erupted across the flesh as the knife separated the skin. Jodie winced and immediately realised her mistake: *how am I going to use my fucking hand now?*

She scolded herself for not cutting her forearm, instead

just falling back to what she'd seen people do in the movies. *Stupid!*

Trying to ignore the pain, Jodie moved her hand over the soul vessel, blood freely dripping down. She held her hand in place for a moment, letting several droplets fall. Some hit the metal latticework, but many fell through the gaps and landed atop the surface of the orb. She watched in fascination as the light inside grew stronger, then she saw a plume of something seep down from the top, like dye in water getting diluted.

It's my blood, she realised. Though Jodie couldn't understand how, the blood had somehow seeped *into* the orb and was being pulled to the centre. She kept her hand in place, allowing more of her blood to drip onto it, still trying to push the stinging pain from her mind.

The light at the centre of the vessel grew more intense, spreading out as more of the blood was pulled in, until soon the entire orb was glowing light blue. Eventually, her blood seemed to stop seeping through the glass surface, and what was inside had been completely absorbed by the light.

Is it finished? she wondered. After waiting a few more moments with no change, she assumed it had to be, so she quickly focused on the remaining ritual, bringing the final one to the top. The action caused her to smear blood across the paper, but she ignored that and read over the final rite:

Ritual of Imprisonment (Kara'meth An'dural).

Zurekai ven tosh-rah,

Durakai esh navahn oru.

Kal-vora menith garah,

Neth'val an'soru, et'vak to'nah

Then the phonetic version:

ZOO-ray-kai ven TOSH-rah

DOO-rah-kai esh nah-VAHN OH-roo

KAHL-voh-rah MEN-ith GAH-rah

NETH-vahl ahn-SOH-roo, et-VAHK toh-NAH

And finally the translation:

Now be chained within,

Your name unspoken and withheld.

In the dark your hatred stilled,

I close the gate, I break your hold.

As she readied herself to speak, the sounds around Jodie fell silent, blinking out in an instant. It left behind only a brief echo that soon faded to nothing as well.

She slowly brought her eyes up, glancing over at the broken windows. There was nothing outside anymore. Then, she looked ahead. The ghostly handyman and the other ghosts were gone… and Jodie's stomach sank at what had replaced them.

Nathaniel Barrow was standing just inside the doorway, silently watching.

28

JOE LAY IN COMPLETE DARKNESS, FIGHTING THE PAIN, STILL unable to move. Breathing was difficult. He felt lightheaded, weak, and woozy. There was no question he was dying—the wound in his side had bled too much.

With him alone and without the lantern, he had feared some of the spirits would show up after Barrow had left him behind. Yet he remained alone, forced to listen to the deathly wails of the dead emanate from somewhere below.

Those wails had fallen silent now, though, and he had no idea why. *What does that mean? Has Jodie failed?*

He desperately hoped she hadn't.

But he knew even if Jodie *did* manage to complete the rites, there was no way she would be able to get help out there in time to save him. He simply didn't have that long left. His only goal now was to hang on long enough to find out if she succeeded. If not, he would join the dead at Parson Hall.

Joe knew if Jodie was successful, her life would change forever. She would get what he had coveted, whether she wanted it or not. Those in charge would have no choice in the matter now. Not once the *Ritual of Imprisonment* was complete.

That ritual had initially been his ace card, the thing he'd intended to use to force the matter after the group he'd wanted to work for had turned their backs on him.

But he'd failed.

Yet another fuck-up, Joe. Just one more in a life of failure.

This is a fitting end for you.

He thought again of Gemma.

I'm so, so sorry.

29

AFTER CRYING OUT, JODIE CLAMPED A BLOODY HAND TO HER head at the sudden agony that burst from within it. The dark spirit continued staring, its mere gaze somehow causing Jodie immense pain.

She tried to look down at the page, yet it was hard to focus, hard to ignore the throbbing in her head. Though she could see the words, for some reason it was difficult to form them aloud.

How is it doing that? It was like the entity was hijacking her mind and fracturing it.

Through all the stabbing pain, she then heard something. No, that was wrong. It wasn't a sound. Not really. But there was a voice in her head nonetheless.

A voice that was not her own.

'She has noticed you.'

There was the enigmatic 'she' again.

'W… who?!' Jodie demanded, both hands now pressed to her head.

'Mother.'

Even in her pain, Jodie was confused. Her first thought

was of Helen, her own mother, but that made no sense at all. It had to be someone else. *Or something else,* she realised.

She stared again at the pages in her hand, trying to see through bleary eyes, willing her mind to focus on the ritual.

'Zurekai… ven… tosh-rah,' she managed to utter. The agony in her head increased, and she dropped to her knees. 'Durakai… esh navahn… oru,' she managed to continue.

More pain. She cried out again. Then she noticed blood dropping onto the page. She quickly wiped the back of her hand across her nose and saw it came away slick with blood.

What the hell is happening?

'Kal-vora… menith… garah.'

The pain was almost unbearable. She screamed again, clenched her teeth, trying to hold it all together.

With a monumental effort, she managed to complete the rite: 'Neth'val an'soru… et'vak… to'nah.' But that was only the first pass of three that was needed.

Jodie heard a roar from ahead. The pain that followed in her head felt like the spike of a pickaxe had been driven straight through her skull. She leaned to the side and vomited. When she looked up she saw Barrow was closer now, having bridged half the gap. Yet he still remained motionless.

She vomited again, stricken with terror, but knew she needed to find it within herself to keep going somehow. She tried to fight against the pain, against the confusion that was clouding her. Then, seemingly out of nowhere, she thought of her mother and of Mark, remembering them both in happier times. The memories seemed to jump out of the void of her mind without prompting, almost in response to what she was feeling.

Though she was still in agony, remembering her mother's smile, and being held by Mark, brought strength back to her.

Jodie began again.

'Zurekai ven tosh-rah.' She took a breath. 'Durakai… esh navahn oru.' There was another roar. Another explosion of pain. 'Kal-vora menith… garah.' Barrow was closer now, only a few feet away. 'Neth'val an'soru… et'vak… to'nah.'

Jodie felt a liquid dribble from her ears as her nose continued to run like a tap, a pool of blood forming on the floor below her. She reached out a shaking hand, taking hold of the soul vessel, holding it up before herself as she prepared for the final verse. The pain increased, and she knew if she didn't get through the rite quickly, her brain would be completely scrambled. This was her last shot.

She glanced up. Barrow was right in front of her now, the entity's awful form looming over her. It was no longer smiling; instead, its lip curled in an expression of loathing.

'Zurekai ven tosh-rah. Durakai… esh—'

Jodie was suddenly thrown back. She didn't feel a blow, yet a force she couldn't explain slammed into her and sent her skidding across the floor, making her head spin. As she tried to regain her bearings, she realised that while she still held the vessel, she'd dropped the papers, though the end of the line she'd started was still fresh in her mind. 'Navahn… oru,' she finished in a slurred voice. Yet even in her disoriented state she knew she needed the sheet with the final two lines of the rite.

Jodie tried to sit up, but her equilibrium was so off she could barely lift her head, finally letting it drop back to the floor, causing a fresh pain to bloom in the back of her skull.

You have to keep going!

While on her back, she felt the blood that had been flowing from her nose building up inside, forcing her to swallow down the thick, metallic taste.

Nathaniel Barrow stood above her again, red-eyed gaze burrowing into her mind. Jodie moved her free hand, searching for the sheets that she'd dropped, yet her fingers only found the stone floor. She tried to move her body but couldn't. Everything hurt too much. Her nose continued to gush, and blood ran from her ears.

Jodie wanted to cry. The stare from the dark spirit and the pain it brought with it was relentless, the Watcher's gaze breaking her mind more and more with each passing second.

Trying to use whatever sanity of hers remained, Jodie tried to recall the rite she was mid-way through. Remembering the last two lines was her only chance of survival.

She searched her mind, knowing if she wasn't about to lose her sanity, remembering wouldn't have been a problem —she'd said it twice already. But as it was, the words were lost behind a fog of madness and pain.

The dark spirit leaned down, its eyes drawing closer, and through them, an image of an eternal void emerged in Jodie's mind—an endless nothing that was not quite empty.

Something resided there. Something horrifying.

Think! Jodie commanded herself, clinging to the last bit of her focus, trying desperately to penetrate the fog.

'Kal-vora,' she began as a shard of memory came through. She saw the entity's head draw back in surprise. Suddenly, more came to her: 'Menith garah!'

The spirit frowned and howled in anger.

'Neth'val an'soru,' Jodie began, remembering more clearly now, yet before she could finish the last line, the spirit thrust its long arms out towards Jodie and clamped its hands around her head.

They squeezed. The pain was immense, forcing her eyes shut. In that instant, she knew her head would burst open like a ripe melon in mere moments.

However, with the last of her strength, she managed to choke out the final words: 'Et'vak… to'nah.'

She waited, still in absolute agony. Nothing happened. *I failed,* she told herself, realising she'd done something wrong.

In that moment, she finally gave up and waited for the inevitable.

But after a beat, the pressure eased.

Jodie opened her eyes. The dark entity was still there, its eyes still wide, staring, but the incessant chipping at Jodie's mind had ceased. Slowly, the entity's arms went slack, the hands falling away from Jodie's head. The lingering, throbbing pain remained, but the immediate agony had relented. Jodie continued to look up at Nathaniel, breath held, fully expecting something else to happen or the spirit to lash out again.

But as she looked up at it, she noticed the light from the lantern started to actually seep through the entity's form, making it look less whole, becoming more like a projection.

Then Nathaniel Barrow dissipated before Jodie's very eyes, turning to something resembling smoke and tiny black particles. Those particles swirled in the air before being drawn downwards. Jodie closed her eyes once more to keep the mist from getting inside; she felt it coat her, feeling like a fine, cold rain.

Then, to her utter shock... things settled. Jodie opened her eyes again. The mist was gone. She forced herself up to her elbows, looking down the length of her body, expecting to see a black film coat her, but there was nothing.

However, her attention was soon drawn to the soul vessel she still held with her right hand. The orb inside wasn't blue anymore, and it no longer glowed.

It was jet black.

30

JODIE ALLOWED HERSELF A LITTLE WHILE BEFORE SHE EVEN attempted to get back to her feet. Her head still throbbed, but the bleeding from her nose and ears had stopped.

The lantern continued to burn, but the flame was now a gently flickering orange. On top of that, she saw the needle in the shard compass was no longer glowing. In fact, it was no longer moving at all.

No other spirits emerged, and the surrounding atmosphere had a stillness she had not felt since arriving.

It... it worked.

Even so, that was still hard for Jodie to accept after being so sure she was going to die.

When she eventually felt strong enough, she stood, grabbing the lantern again. She looked at the items on the floor and briefly wondered if she should pack them up—specifically the soul vessel, which seemed to call to her. However, looking at the items also made her think of their owner.

Joe!

Jodie took off running, remembering the shape he'd been

up in the attic, barely able to get his words out and lying in a pool of blood.

She briefly hesitated when coming out of the hall, just in case something still remained, but once she saw the coast was clear, she continued on, demanding more from her tired, aching body. As she ran, Jodie felt an odd sensation. It was a kind of pull, something that made her want to return to the old hall, a nagging feeling that she'd left something important behind. *The soul vessel... it's calling out to me.* Part of her wanted to go back and claim it, but she pushed on, not sure why it had popped up in her mind.

Her vision was still a little blurry, and she felt lightheaded, but Jodie was able to navigate her way up the stairs to the next floor before dashing to the stairwell to the attic.

Eventually, she burst through into the main attic space and spotted Joe still lying where he had been on the floor. He slowly turned his head to face her, looking pained, but a flash of relief washed over him, followed by a weak smile.

'You... you did it?' he asked, not hiding the surprise in his voice. Jodie ran over to him and knelt down, shocked at the amount of blood beneath him and how much had soaked through the clothes at his abdomen.

'Are you okay?' she asked, concerned, immediately realising that was a stupid thing to ask. *Of course he isn't okay.*

'What... what happened?' Joe went on, ignoring her question. 'I heard... things.'

'I... I did it,' Jodie replied. 'I finished the ritual. Even bled to get the job done. See?' She lifted her hand to show him her stinging palm. Joe studied it.

'So... it's over?' he asked and coughed again.

Jodie nodded. 'I think so. The soul vessel turned black after Barrow had just... vanished. Does that sound like it worked?'

Joe let out a sigh and let his head fall back against the

floor. 'Yeah,' he said with obvious relief. 'Yeah, it does.' He winced in pain, then turned his eyes sideways to look at Jodie's raised hand again. 'You shouldn't have cut… your palm,' he said, struggling for breath. 'It'll stop you… using your hand.'

'I know that now,' Jodie said with a smile. 'Where were you with that advice ten minutes ago?'

Joe took another deep breath. 'Dying… I guess,' he said, glancing down the length of his body.

Jodie leaned forward. 'You're not dying,' she said, then fear shot through her. 'Are you?'

He gave her a rueful smile. 'I'm not doing great… Jodie,' he replied.

In response, Jodie quickly got to her feet. 'Then I need to get you some help. Do you have a phone or something I can use? Or should I go and fetch—'

'Jodie, wait,' Joe interrupted, raising his hand. 'Just… wait.'

'But you need *help!*' Jodie stressed, looking back towards the door, already trying to work out where she could go to get it. *I'll need to drive into town and just wake someone up.*

'It's too late,' Joe said. Jodie turned to him with a frown.

'What… what do you mean?'

'I'm… not… going to make it.'

'Of course you will!' Jodie exclaimed, squatting down beside him again. She took his hand. 'Just hold on. I'll fix this.'

'I need you… to listen,' Joe went on. 'Please. This… this is important.'

'But—'

'*No,*' he insisted, raising his voice but causing another brief coughing fit. 'Jodie, just… listen. If you… imprisoned Barrow, then there's someone… I need you to call.'

'Yes, I know, I have to call an ambulance,' Jodie said. 'And the police.'

'Not them!' Joe forced out. 'It's important… you don't call

them,' he went on, his gaze burning sternly. 'I mean it. They… can't help. I'll be dead by the time… they're here. But'—he lifted his head with obvious strain—'you'll be in trouble if you do call them. You're… the only other one here. With me… dead… you'll be blamed for it.'

Jodie shook her head. 'No, I'll explain,' she said. 'Or think of a lie, or… or—'

'No,' Joe said. 'There's… more. Since you completed the… ritual… then you need… help. It isn't… over, Jodie.'

Jodie recoiled, a single eyebrow raised. 'What do you mean?'

'Too long… to… explain,' Joe forced out, wincing again. His breathing was laboured. 'There's… a phone… in my… car. The code to unlock it… is two-four-nine… three. It's a… burner. There's only one contact in it. Call that… number.'

'But I need to get you—'

Joe squeezed her hand, though his grip was weak. 'It's… okay,' he said—Jodie felt her eyes tearing up. 'Call the number. You'll speak to someone… Mr. Ellerman. Explain… everything. He will… send help.'

'An ambulance?' Jodie asked.

'It's… too late,' Joe said again. His breathing came out in raspy wheezes now. 'You told me before that… you lost your husband, right?'

Jodie paused, then nodded. 'Why?'

'I lost… someone too,' he said, his voice growing weaker. 'I came out here to… try to see them… again.' Joe coughed up a throatful of blood, which coated his face. 'You can see your husband… again. There is… a way.'

Jodie paused in utter shock, trying to process what the dying man had just told her. At first, her words wouldn't come. 'I—I don't understand,' she eventually said. 'What do you mean? How can I see Mark again?'

Joe's hands fell away and his head rolled to the side, eyes

starting to lose focus. 'Just… call,' he managed to wheeze out before his gaze became flat.

'Joe!' Jodie said. She shook him frantically. 'Joe!' She got no response, and after a moment she tentatively held a hand beneath his nose to check for signs of breathing, no matter how weak. There was nothing. 'Joe!' she shouted and shook him again.

The response was the same. Nothing.

Eventually Jodie sat back on her haunches in utter shock, realising she was staring at a dead man.

31

Even after sitting with Joe's lifeless body for over ten minutes, thinking through what he'd just told her, Jodie still hadn't decided what to do.

It all seemed so insane.

On the one hand, she felt calling the police was the correct course of action. Of *course* it was the right course of action. A man was dead. The police needed to know.

And while she *was* worried they might think she was involved in his death, she was sure the evidence would eventually prove otherwise. At least... she was *almost* sure.

But what exactly do I tell them? Jodie asked herself. *How do I explain this?*

That was the issue. The truth just wasn't believable, and nothing else would make sense.

More importantly, it was what Joe had said about seeing Mark again that stuck with Jodie. She wanted to ignore it, to tell herself it wasn't true—*couldn't* be true—but even so...

She'd just experienced a night full of impossibilities.

The longer she dwelt on it, the more Jodie convinced herself it *might* be possible, considering what she'd seen.

The idea of seeing Mark again, maybe even speaking to him… it was all she wanted.

Then there was the vague warning Joe had given her, saying things weren't over and that she *needed* help.

Staring at his lifeless body a little more, Jodie finally made her decision.

You're insane, she told herself as she got to her feet. Insane or not, Jodie started to walk back downstairs, heading for the car outside. Once back in the old hall, however, she felt another nagging pull to get the vessel. She didn't think of grabbing the compass or anything else, just the soul vessel. She couldn't understand why that one item seemed to call out to her.

Ignore it, Jodie told herself as she climbed out of the window. She then headed all the way over to Joe's vehicle, the rear doors of which were still open. She began searching, and soon came upon a small, black flip-phone in the side pocket of one of the duffle bags. She opened the phone and found it was turned off.

Jodie quickly wondered if it had died in the pulse just like hers had, but given it was switched off and several dozen yards from the house, she hoped that wasn't the case. Besides, Joe had sent her out there to get it, so surely he'd been confident it hadn't been fried. She pushed the duffle bag farther across and sat on the rear seat of the vehicle, closing the door behind her. She then held her finger on the power button long enough for the phone to come to life.

Thank God.

After that, she tapped in the code Joe had given her to unlock everything and managed to find her way to the contact list. As expected, there was a single contact.

Mr. Ellerman.

It all seemed ominous to her, so Jodie allowed herself a

moment to second guess, just to make certain she was doing the right thing. Finally, she hit dial.

The phone rang once, then connected.

'Mr. Hurst,' came a stern male voice. 'You stole from us. Where are you?' The man sounded mature. Not ancient, but hardly a spring chicken.

'Is this Mr. Ellerman?' Jodie asked.

There was a pause. 'Who is this?' the man asked. He was well spoken, and if Jodie was to guess, she'd say he came from money.

'That's... not important,' she replied, hesitant to give her name. 'But Joe said I needed to call you.' Then she waited, hoping the man would say something else.

There was another beat of silence. 'Okay. I need you to listen to me,' he began, losing his sternness. 'There is a chance you are in danger. I need you to get Mr. Hurst and put him on the phone immediately. I'm afraid he might—'

'Joe's dead.'

'He... he's what?'

'Dead,' Jodie repeated.

'Where are you?' the man said, his voice taking on an urgent tone.

Jodie wondered if she should give that information, realising once she did, someone would likely come for her. *But that's the whole point of the call,* she reminded herself. Even so, it still took her a second to divulge the information. 'Parson Hall,' she began. 'It's in—'

'I know it,' the man said. 'I need to ask you a question, miss, and I'm aware it may sound strange, but believe me when I tell you, it's extremely important. Do you happen to know if Joe performed any kind of strange... activity... at the property before—'

'He started the rituals,' Jodie confirmed, interrupting him. 'Summoned the dark spirit, and it killed him.'

She heard the man swallow. 'Jesus,' he uttered. 'Okay, Miss, is there a strange-looking lantern close to you by any chance? If so—'

'It's all taken care of,' Jodie said, interrupting yet again.

'What do you mean?'

'I mean I finished it. I carried out the remaining rites. Spilled my blood on that soul vessel. Imprisoned the spirit. It's done. I saw the vessel turn black just after the entity disappeared in front of me.'

The silence stretched even longer this time. '*You* did all that?' he eventually asked.

'I did,' Jodie said. 'I mean, I had Joe's notes to help me, but yes.'

'And where was Mr. Hurst when all that happened?'

Jodie took a breath. 'Dying,' she replied. 'He was… injured… and couldn't get up. After it was finished, I went back to him and he insisted that I call you. He said… well, he said I still needed help. Something about it not being over.'

'That is… unfortunately true, I'm afraid.'

'What does that mean?' Jodie asked. 'How is it not over? It's finished here, the spirit is gone. I can just go back to my life now, right?'

'I'll explain everything when we get there, I promise,' the man said. 'I know you might be tempted to flee, and I can completely understand that, but *if* you stay I'll give you all the answers you need. What's more, Mr. Hurst was right. You were involved with the imprisonment, so there is no running from this. Not anymore.'

'Is that a threat of some kind?' Jodie asked. 'A warning because I know too much?'

'It is not,' Mr. Ellerman explained. 'It has nothing to do with me. It's the ritual itself. You are connected now. Again, I'll explain more when I get there. Please, just allow me the chance to give you answers.'

'Joe said something else,' Jodie quickly cut in. 'Said he was doing all this because he wanted to see someone he lost. He thinks it's possible to find loved ones that died. Is that... is that right?'

'Have you lost someone?'

'That's... not the point,' Jodie said, but knew her desperate tone had given her away.

'It is possible, yes,' the man said. 'Give me a half hour to get there. Can I count on you to wait?'

Now it was Jodie's turn to pause as she thought things over. 'I'll be here,' she eventually confirmed. 'Just hurry.'

She then hung up and was left alone with her thoughts. *What am I doing? This is insane.*

Regardless, it was done. The wheels were set in motion. Sure, she could run, but that wouldn't bring answers. And it also wouldn't help her against the mysterious lingering threat Joe had warned her about.

So, as promised, she waited, staying in the car and growing more and more restless with each passing moment. The next twenty-five minutes passed with agonising slowness, but eventually she saw two sets of headlights approaching down the long road five minutes earlier than promised.

Jodie exited the SUV to make herself visible as the other vehicles came to a stop near her. They were identical: both a sleek black with fully tinted windows. The engines continued running as the doors opened. Four people emerged from the first and three from the second. Jodie's eyes were immediately drawn to the older man that got out of the passenger side of the front vehicle.

He appeared to be somewhere in his sixties and was dressed in a black overcoat, but beneath that he wore a smart grey suit complete with suit-vest. He also had on a grey fedora, which the man removed as soon as his light-blue eyes fell on Jodie. He had a full head of brushed back hair, though it was completely silver.

Jodie assumed this was Mr. Ellerman. He had a thin face with small jowls on either side of his mouth and was clean-shaven. The man also had a prominent but thin nose and thick eyebrows that still held some black in with the grey.

'I assume you are the lady I spoke to on the phone,' he said with a pleasant, if hesitant, smile.

'Yes,' Jodie replied. She wasn't sure if she should hold out her hand to greet him, so instead settled on just introducing herself. 'My name is Jodie.'

He gave a polite nod. 'I am Percival Ellerman. And first of all, I'm so sorry you were caught up in all of this. It should never have happened.'

'You've got that right,' Jodie said. '*None* of this should have happened. Joe coming out here in the first place was irresponsible.'

'It was,' the man agreed.

Jodie tilted her head in confusion. 'Then… why sanction it? Why send him in the first place?'

'We didn't,' Mr. Ellerman responded, catching Jodie off guard.

'What do you mean? Joe worked for you… right?'

But the man slowly shook his head. 'We were training him, getting him ready,' Mr. Ellerman began. 'However, we soon found Mr. Hurst to be compulsive and rash. A little too… headstrong. We had misgivings about him, so we decided to cut him loose.'

'Cut him loose?'

'That's right,' the man said. 'We stopped the training and told him to go back to his old life. But… he didn't take kindly to that. He stole some things from us last week and we've been trying to find him since. I was worried he would try something like he did tonight.'

He turned to the others and pointed off towards the building. All but two began to move, with the remaining men staying close to Mr. Ellerman. *Bodyguards,* Jodie realised.

'Where are they going?' Jodie asked, nodding to the others—one woman and three men—that headed into Parson Hall.

'To secure the building,' Mr. Ellerman said. 'I don't doubt what you told me is true, that the spirit is imprisoned—because you honestly wouldn't be alive otherwise. But we just need to make sure everything is safe.'

'Joe is in there,' she said. 'His body, I mean.'

Mr. Ellerman gave a remorseful nod. 'We'll collect him.'

'Collect him and do what?' Jodie asked with a questioning gaze.

'Bury him, of course,' the man replied, as if it were the most obvious thing in the world. 'Unfortunately, Mr. Hurst didn't have anyone left in his life, so we're the ones who will ensure he at least gets a proper burial.'

'Oh,' Jodie replied, having for some reason expected a different answer—something more nefarious. 'And you said Joe was… rash?'

Mr. Ellerman nodded. 'Yes, very. We made the decision not to proceed with him, as I said, though it soon became apparent he wasn't going to accept that. Tonight is just further evidence that our decision was the right one. Anything could have happened out here, and innocent people could have died. People like yourself.'

Jodie instinctively wanted to defend Joe, despite not really knowing him that well. After all, he hadn't *intended* to put her in danger. Indeed, he'd tried to steer her clear of that. But even so, Joe had been reckless, so the old man's words did ring true.

'Well, thankfully I'm okay,' Jodie said. 'But Joe… I don't know what happened exactly, only that the spirit killed him, but it looked like it was a painful way to go. He didn't deserve that.'

'No,' the man said. 'I agree with that. Despite my misgivings and our disagreements, I didn't want harm to come to him.' Mr. Ellerman glanced over at the building for a moment. 'Which brings us to the most important question… Jodie, right?'

'Right. So, what *is* the most important question?'

His eyes then settled on her. 'What do we do next?'

She studied him for a moment. 'Well, what are the options? Would you let me go if I wanted to?'

'We couldn't very well detain you,' the man said. 'We have no authority over you so of course we would. But if you did want to go, I'd like a little time to get things cleared away here, so there is no trace back to me or my team.'

'And if I said no to that and just ran?' Jodie asked, curious rather than antagonistic.

'Then I suppose we would have to work fast. But… there are questions you need answers to. We both know that. And I wasn't lying, you *are* in danger, you just don't realise it yet.'

'How?' Jodie demanded. 'What did completing that ritual get me involved in? You promised me answers on the phone, so it's time to give them.'

Now it was his turn to study her. 'There is a lot to tell,' Mr. Ellerman said. He turned to his car. 'Come with me. I'll take you somewhere safe to explain everything. What's more, I can show you things that will back up what I'm saying.'

'Come with you?' Jodie asked, folding her arms over her chest. 'You think I trust you enough to jump into a car with you people and go God knows where?'

'I suppose I can't ask for trust like that, you're right,' the man admitted. 'But every minute we're here is a minute we risk someone stumbling across us. I don't want to be here any longer than we absolutely need to. The things I'm going to explain, well, as I said, it will take time. And after that, you'll have a decision to make.'

'A decision?'

Mr. Ellerman nodded. 'Yes. Whether or not you want to take up the mantle we denied Joe.'

Jodie's eyes went wide. 'What? You want me to become a… hunter?'

The man cocked his head. 'How do you know that term?'

'I read Joe's dossier,' Jodie explained.

A look of disappointment fell over Mr. Ellerman's face. 'He let you see his information? That was even more reckless of him.'

'Answer the question,' Jodie pressed, not bothering to correct him. 'Is that what you mean?'

'It is,' the man confirmed. 'The chance to hunt more of these things.'

Jodie couldn't help but laugh. 'Why would I ever want to do that? I don't think I've ever been as scared or in as much danger as I was tonight. On what planet do you think I'd want to do this kind of thing regularly?'

'On this planet,' Mr. Ellerman stated. 'Because doing so will bring you more knowledge… and it'll also bring you closer to the person you lost. I mentioned on the phone there is a way to see the dead again. This is the way. It's why Joe was so desperate to join our ranks.'

Jodie hesitated, trying to take everything in. 'And why are you so keen to get me to join up?' she asked. 'You know nothing about me. If Joe wasn't good enough, what on earth makes you think I'm going to be?'

'In truth?' the man began, 'I don't know if you're suitable. I mean, you *did* imprison one of the dark spirits, which is no easy feat. But it isn't our normal policy to bring people in without seeing what they're capable of.'

'So… what's different with me?'

'Well, for one... because of what you did here tonight,' Mr. Ellerman said. 'You imprisoned an entity without really knowing much about it. That's impressive. However, in doing so, you started something, so to leave you on your own now would be... irresponsible of us. The only option I see is to train you.'

'But again, what if I don't *want* to be trained?'

'That's your choice. All I'll say is that would be extremely dangerous for you.'

Jodie tilted her head back and repressed a sigh of annoyance. 'Will you just tell me *why* it's dangerous?'

Instead, Mr. Ellerman looked at the vehicle he'd just disembarked from. 'Come with me, Jodie' he said again. 'We'll get you somewhere safe and lay everything out. You can make your choice then.'

'We've been over this,' Jodie said. 'I'm not one for jumping into cars with strangers in the dead of night. I don't know you well enough, and this whole thing is completely nuts, quite frankly.'

'You're not wrong to say that,' Mr. Ellerman said. 'But the circumstances here are... extraordinary, no? Don't think of it as trust, think of it more as... a leap of faith.' Jodie chewed the side of her lip. The answers he promised did sound appealing, yet the sensible side of her remained insistent the whole thing was crazy. 'I'll also explain more about how you can see your lost loved one again,' the man continued.

Jodie stopped chewing. She straightened up. 'But that's impossible,' she said. 'It *has* to be. Surely?'

But the man just shook his head. 'I assure you, it isn't. Don't get me wrong, it won't happen straight away—it will take time—but we can make it come to fruition. Come have a conversation with me, at least. You'd be free to go at any point. But I think when you hear what I have to say, you won't be quick to abandon this chance I'm giving you.'

An image of Mark swam to the fore of Jodie's mind. *Is it really possible?* She tried to fight the temptation, to warn herself off this obvious insanity, but her heart yearned for her love. The chance to see him again, no matter how slim, made her chest ache.

'Well?' the man asked, holding out his hand for her. 'Will you come with us?'

Jodie studied the outstretched hand.

Don't do it! Don't be so stupid!

Jodie took a breath, then… took his hand. 'Fine,' she said. 'I'll take the leap. For now.'

Mr. Ellerman smiled. 'Thank you.' He gestured to the car. 'Please, this way. I promise you, if you're willing to commit to this, you won't regret it.'

Jodie walked with the stranger, flanked by his two bodyguards on either side. All she could think of was Mark.

You're making a mistake, her mind screamed at her. But Jodie got into the car anyway.

TO BE CONTINUED…

DARK SPIRITS: THE CRONE

Bonus content!
Here are the first two chapters from Book 2 in the series.

Dark Spirits: The Crone, coming soon.

CHAPTER 1

JODIE CALLAGHAN SAT IN THE BACK SEAT OF THE SUV WITH her new acquaintance Mr. Percival Ellerman sitting on the other side. Given the size of the vehicle there was plenty of space between them, and a wide leather armrest had been pulled down to cover the middle seat; two crystal glasses of scotch sat in cupholders within the armrest.

There were two men up front and a tinted screen separating the front of the vehicle from the back. While Jodie had no idea if it was soundproof, it at least gave the impression of privacy.

She guessed they had been driving for around forty-five minutes so far, and though there had been some conversation after first setting off, it had quickly waned. Mainly because their brief talk had consisted of Jodie trying to find out more about the insane situation she'd found herself in, with Mr. Ellerman avoiding any direct answers and promising more information was coming when they reached their destination. So, Jodie had resigned herself to simply looking out into the night, watching the scenery move by, impressed by the near-silence of the vehicle.

Though all the windows were tinted, she was still aware of headlights behind them from the other SUV, which contained the rest of the crew Mr. Ellerman had taken with him to Parson Hall.

Joe's belongings are there as well, she thought, allowing herself to go over the events of the past few hours. Part of her felt like it had all just been a dream.

For one, she'd watched a man die. And while it wasn't the first time she'd seen a dead body—the worst moment of her life was waking to find her husband dead beside her—it was the only time she'd watched someone's life actually slip away in real time.

But that had only been the tip of the iceberg. She had also seen things her mind could scarcely comprehend, even though she was a paranormal investigator. Most terrifying had been the spirit of Nathaniel Barrow, with his twisted form and red eyes, as well as the ghosts of his scores of victims.

She had also witnessed those ghosts forced back by a strange lantern with an eerie blue glow. She had seen the dark spirit of Nathaniel Barrow trapped in a glass ball Joe had called a soul vessel. To top it all off, she herself had carried out incantations in a foreign tongue and had brought the whole nightmare to an end.

Jodie thought of Joe once more. While she hadn't known him for more than a few hours, they'd been through an intense experience together, which had made them feel closer than they really had been. He was important to her, somehow. His death sat like a lead weight in Jodie's gut. She didn't mourn him exactly, but there was still a sense of loss.

Her hand continued to throb, and she looked down to inspect the wound across her palm. She'd cut herself as part of the ritual, but was still annoyed at slicing her palm—any movement at all made pain shoot through her hand. Thankfully, the wound had long-since stopped bleeding, though she knew it still needed to be cleaned.

After another fifteen minutes of travelling, she turned to Mr. Ellerman, who she noticed was checking his watch. *He's done that a few times now.* It was as if he was anxious about something, in a hurry to get back.

She wondered how long their meeting would go on for, and what time she'd finally be allowed to leave.

'What will you do with Joe's car?' she asked.

Mr. Ellerman turned to her with a raised eyebrow. 'What do you mean?'

'It's at Parson Hall. I'm guessing you can't just leave it there.'

The man shook his head. 'Don't worry, I already have someone going to retrieve it. And when we are finished with our discussion, we can take you back to get *your* vehicle as well.'

'But… what if someone finds it in the meantime?'

The elderly man shook his head again. 'They won't,' he said with confidence. 'Hardly anyone ever goes out there. We've done our research.'

'Well, Joe and I ended up there at the same time,' Jodie said.

Mr. Ellerman laughed. 'True. But I think your car will be okay for a little while longer.'

Jodie thought about it, then accepted what he'd said. Besides, she was far too eager to find out what he had to share than to worry about her vehicle further.

Eventually, the two-car convoy turned onto a dark, winding road, and after a few hundred meters hit another turn off, this one gated.

The gates were already open, so both vehicles entered

then continued down a long driveway of smooth asphalt. From her position in the back, and with the tinted screen in front of her, Jodie wasn't able to see what lay ahead, though she imagined it was a house of some kind. Given the secluded area and the size of the grounds around her, she expected it to be a looming, stately home.

However, when the car eventually stopped and the two men in the front disembarked and opened her door for her, she was… surprised.

The house *was* large, but only in footprint, given it was a single storey. Rather than seeming grand, it almost came across as lost, with the trees around shielding the dwelling and the wall-climbing plants helping the house blend in with its surroundings.

'Expecting something… *more?*' Mr. Ellerman asked with an amused expression.

'I… no,' Jodie replied. 'Not at all. It's a really lovely house.'

'It serves our purpose,' the older man said. 'A nice place for me to reside as I handle operations up here.'

'Operations?' Jodie asked.

He gave a small chuckle. 'I'll explain in good time, as I will everything else. Why don't we go inside first and get settled? It's early and you haven't slept. I'm guessing you could do with a cup of coffee?'

Jodie nodded. 'That or a good sleep.'

'I notice you avoided the scotch in the car. That might have calmed your nerves.'

'Not really my thing,' Jodie said, curling her lip. 'Hate the taste.'

She glanced around and saw the second car was parked behind them, with the passengers already disembarked. The sole woman in the group held Joe's duffle bag in her hands. As Jodie stared at it, she felt something. A distinct pull. It was the same sensation she'd experienced back at Parson Hall, when she'd been outside and Joe's artefacts had still been inside.

'Shall we?' Mr. Ellerman said, gesturing towards the house. Jodie regarded him, hesitant, again wondering if she'd made a mistake by coming here with him.

The man had seemed friendly enough. She guessed the gaunt man was in his sixties and he had a prominent nose and thick eyebrows. His face was weathered, but even so, his eyes shone with a kind of vibrance that defied his advanced years.

Jodie also glanced at the other people present: a team of seven that screamed security, especially since they were all dressed in dark colours and hadn't said anything the whole time she'd been around them. Even so, Jodie had never once felt threatened—in fact, after letting her out of the vehicle moments ago, two of the men had given her a courteous nod.

Part of her still wanted to turn and run, acknowledging how insane she was for coming out here in the first place. But another part of her urged her to listen to Joe's warning about needing help.

Plus… she dearly wanted to know if Mr. Ellerman was telling the truth about her being able to one day see Mark again.

I'll hear him out, and if he's full of shit I'll just leave.

She noticed the man check his watch again. Jodie frowned. 'Late for something?' she asked.

He lowered his hand and shook his head, smiling. 'Not at all. Just like to keep on top of time.'

Jodie wasn't buying it. There was a *reason* he was constantly checking, and it added another checkmark to her 'get the hell out of there' column. Still, she held firm, her need to know outweighing her caution.

Mr. Ellerman motioned towards the house again. 'I assure you the coffee I have is first rate,' he said.

Despite her hesitation, Jodie replied, 'Then I'll take milk and two sugars, please.'

They both set off. As she walked, Jodie stared at the house ahead, wondering what secrets were about to be revealed.

CHAPTER 2

The entrance hallway was warm, *really* warm, with the heat hitting Jodie like a wall as she walked inside from the night's chill. Mr. Ellerman quickly shook off his overcoat and hung it on a rack, then held his hand out to take Jodie's. Given the frantic exertions of that night she wasn't sure she wanted to take it off, knowing she likely reeked. But her internal debate was short-lived—*I'll probably pass out from the heat if I keep it on.*

After handing over her coat, she and the older man moved deeper into the space to allow the others to enter as well, though Jodie noticed that only four of them did, with the remaining three waiting outside, including the woman with the bag.

The entrance hall was lit with wall-mounted fittings, and the illumination cast from them was weak with a warm hue. The walls had timber panels up to the halfway point, with plaster above. Many paintings were fixed there, showing landscapes as well as portraits of people Jodie didn't recognise. The floor was timber, though there was also a thick red rug running down its length. There were six panelled doors off the hall, all dense oak.

'You all live here?' Jodie asked.

'My friends here stay at the house when on duty,' Mr. Ellerman replied. 'But I'm the only full-time resident.'

'And you own the house?'

The man shook his head. 'Not exactly. It belongs to the organisation.'

What organisation? Jodie wanted to ask, but knew answers were coming. 'Looks like capturing spirits is a lucrative business, then, if you're staying in a place like this.'

Mr. Ellerman chuckled but shook his head. 'Not at all. We don't do this for money. Our goals are much more... important.'

'Really?' Jodie asked. 'Care to tell me how?'

'I will,' he said. 'But I don't want to get ahead of myself. Rest assured, when I've explained everything, I have a feeling you'll want to join us in our mission. In fact, I'm sure of it.'

Jodie took a moment to process his words. 'Then let's get to it.'

Mr. Ellerman smiled and motioned to a door on their left. 'Through there.'

Jodie took a step forward... then paused. Her vision suddenly started to swim and she almost stumbled, her equilibrium off kilter. She felt a steadying hand take hold of her shoulder.

'Are you okay, Jodie?' Mr. Ellerman asked.

Almost as soon as it had come over her, the dizziness passed. 'I... yeah,' she replied, confused. 'I'm fine. I think.' She shook her head. 'I don't know what happened. I guess I'm just... exhausted.' Jodie turned her eyes to Mr. Ellerman and saw he was studying her intently.

'Let's get you seated,' he said. 'The coffee might help perk you up.'

Mr. Ellerman led her through the door and into a large sitting room, all the while keeping a watchful eye on her as she walked. However, Jodie once again felt strong on her feet.

Like the hallway, the lighting in the room was low, given off only by a central chandelier. There were multiple elegant low sofas, all with green upholstery and dark oak legs. In addition, there were side tables and bookshelves, and close to the fireplace was a coffee table with two sofas around it. That was the area Jodie was guided over to.

She took a seat close to the unlit fire and her host sat down ninety-degrees to her.

'You sure you're okay?' Mr. Ellerman asked.

Jodie gave a quick nod. 'Yeah. Just felt a little… odd. But it passed pretty quickly. Like I said, I'm probably just tired from everything that happened tonight.'

'Understandable,' the man said. 'You've been through a lot. It's bound to have taken its toll. Would you like something other than coffee? Some painkillers, perhaps?'

Jodie shook her head. 'Just a coffee will be fine,' she said. No sooner had she spoken than she felt her stomach bubble and cramp.

Mr. Ellerman cocked his head to the side. 'You're sweating.' He pointed to her forehead and Jodie immediately brought a hand up to her brow, which was damp. 'We can talk a little later, if that helps,' he went on. 'You can rest here for a while until you feel up to it. I can give you some privacy.'

'I'm okay,' Jodie insisted, even though she knew that wasn't quite true. She felt… off. On edge. Jittery. But those were all signs of fatigue, so she figured there was nothing to worry about. *I can rest later.*

'You're sure?' Mr. Ellerman asked.

'Certain,' Jodie replied. 'Let's just get started. Tell me all you need to. As I said earlier, I want to know *everything*.'

Mr. Ellerman smiled, but his eyes moved over to the door. 'Please bring in the refreshments,' he called. The door opened immediately and a man Jodie hadn't seen before entered, carrying a silver tray. The tray held a teapot, a cafetiere full of coffee, mugs, teacups, a jug of milk, a bowl of sugar, and a plate of biscuits.

The man himself looked to be in his forties, with dark, brushed-back hair and a pale complexion. He was thin and dressed in a smart black suit. With his widow's peak, Jodie couldn't help but think he looked like a vampire.

'That was fast,' she said. 'Was he just… waiting outside for you to shout?'

Mr. Ellerman nodded. 'I had one of the others message ahead when we were close, so Mr. Cullen here prepared our refreshments in advance.'

'Efficient,' Jodie said as Mr. Cullen set the tray down on the coffee table.

'Will there be anything else, sir?' the man asked, voice smooth.

'Not for the moment, Alexander, thank you.'

Mr. Cullen then gave a courteous nod, straightened up, and left, quietly closing the door behind him on his way out.

Mr. Ellerman leaned forward and started to pour the drinks. When he started adding milk to Jodie's coffee, he glanced up at her. 'Say when.'

'That's good,' Jodie told him after he'd added a healthy portion.

'It was two sugars, right?'

Jodie nodded. 'Please.'

Once her drink was ready, the man set her mug down before her and then started to prepare his own tea.

'So,' Jodie began. 'Don't keep me in suspense any longer. I

think I'm owed some answers.' She took a sip of her drink, which was surprisingly good. In that moment, she lamented not being more of a coffee connoisseur, knowing she always killed any natural flavours with milk and sugar.

'That's fair,' Mr. Ellerman said as he sat back. 'I suppose I should start with the most obvious thing. Namely, who we are and what we do.'

'Yeah,' Jodie agreed. 'I mean, I have an idea. You guys hunt those dark spirts, right?'

'Well, if we're boiling it down to basics, then yes, I suppose that's right. Though there is more to it.'

'How so?' Jodie asked, leaning forward and placing her elbows on her knees, fingers interlocked. 'Because I think…' She then paused and frowned, blinking. Her vision had blurred and her head swam once again.

'Ms. Callaghan?' Mr. Ellerman asked.

'I… I… uh…' Yet Jodie found it hard to think clearly. Her skin tingled and her head was throbbing. *What's wrong with me?*

Jodie saw movement in her periphery, but it was hard to focus. She realised Mr. Ellerman was waving a hand in front of her eyes to draw her attention.

'I'm… fine,' she said, though she brought her hand up to her temples with a wince as the throbbing turned into pain.

Mr. Ellerman stood up. 'Please wait here,' he said. 'I'll get you some pain medication.'

'I don't need it,' Jodie answered, shaking her head. 'I'm just tired.'

'I insist,' the man said, striding over to the door. The pain in Jodie's head was familiar, just like what she'd experienced back at Parson Hall. She wondered if it was the aftereffect of dealing with the dark spirit or something entirely unrelated. She recalled how her mind had nearly broken under its gaze, and how it had even caused her nose and ears to run with blood. *Maybe it damaged my brain?*

When Jodie heard the door close, she was almost certain she heard a follow-up *click.*

Did... did he lock it?

But that didn't make sense to her. *Why would he lock me in?*

After taking a moment to steady herself, Jodie forced herself to her feet, thankful she was still able to stand despite the dizziness. She then made her way over to the door and tried the handle.

It didn't open.

A stab of panic pierced her chest. She tried again, getting the same result. Jodie banged on the door. 'Hey, what the hell? Open up!' She continued to thump on the thick wood with the side of her fist. No response came. Jodie cursed herself for being so stupid as to come out there in the first place. *What were you thinking, Jodie?*

She yanked and yanked at the handle. 'Open up. *Now!* This isn't funny!'

Still no reply. Realising she wasn't going to accomplish anything, she turned and ran over to one of the tall windows that looked out over the dark grounds. The windows were sash style with Georgian bars separating the panes of glass. Jodie bent down to try to lift the bottom section, but before she'd even begun to heave she saw a lock in place on the side of the frame. Her heart raced as she grabbed the bottom sash regardless and tried to slide it up. It was futile.

Jodie then turned back to the door. 'I'm going to break this goddamn window if you don't let me out!' she called with both panic and anger swirling through her. There was still no response. 'You hear me?!'

Jodie kicked out at a side table close to her, knocking it over and smashing the vase perched atop it. Teeth gritted, she gazed at the fallen table, trying to determine if it was heavy enough to use to break the panes of glass.

Should be, she thought. *But... then what?*

Ultimately, Jodie had no idea where she was, given she'd been chauffeured for quite a while in the dark. *Where would I even run to?*

On top of that, she doubted those that had trapped her in the room would just let her waltz away unchallenged.

Once again, she scolded herself for being so naïve as to have gotten into the car in the first place. *You stupid fucking idiot, Jodie!*

But even as she thought it, her mind ran back to Joe, who had insisted she call Mr. Ellerman, telling her she would need the man's help.

Did Joe know something like this would happen? That they would trap me?

While Jodie didn't know Joe well, her gut told her he wouldn't have set her up like that.

Regardless, she knew she couldn't just stay there and wait for whatever Ellerman had planned. She leaned down and grabbed the side table.

As she did, the lights blew, plunging the room into darkness.

Jodie whipped her head round in shock at the sudden *pops*. Her body tensed and her mind raced to try to figure out *why* the bulbs had all exploded at the same time. She hoped to find a rational explanation. *An electrical surge, maybe?*

Her initial reaction was that Mr. Ellerman had somehow caused it, but she couldn't work out how. Jodie's grip on the table slackened as she stared into the shadows, feeling vulnerable and exposed. Thankfully, it wasn't *completely* dark, so the moonlight that came in through the windows allowed her to see a few feet before her. But beyond that, there was nothing. She turned to the window again, her mind telling her to follow through with the plan of breaking it to escape. If the others came for her, so be it.

Yet before she could, she heard a raspy breath from the far side of the room. Jodie gasped and looked ahead, staring deep into the shadows.

Her gasp turned into a scream as she saw two familiar red eyes hanging in the dark. Her head then exploded in agony.

WHAT TO READ NEXT...

EAGER OR MORE?

Haunted: Perron Manor

Book 1 in the Haunted Series.

Sisters Sarah and Chloe inherit a house they could never have previously dreamed of owning. It seems too good to be true.

Shortly after they move in, however, the siblings start to notice strange things: horrible smells, sudden drops in temperature, as well as unexplainable sounds and feelings of being watched.

All of that is compounded when they find a study upstairs, filled with occult items and a strange book written in Latin.

Their experiences grow more frequent and more terrifying, building towards a heart-stopping climax where the sisters come face to face with the evil behind Perron Manor. Will they survive and save their very souls?

Buy Haunted: Perron Manor now.

FREE BOOK

Sign up to my mailing list for free books...

Want more dark stories? Sign up to my mailing list and receive the free ebooks: *The Nightmare Collection - Vol 1* as well as *Inside: Perron Manor* (a prequel novella to *Haunted: Perron Manor*).

The novel-length short story collection and prequel novella are sure to have you sleeping with the lights on.

Sign up now.

www.leemountford.com

OTHER BOOKS BY LEE MOUNTFORD

The Supernatural Horror Collection

The Demonic
The Mark
Forest of the Damned

The Extreme Horror Collection

Horror in the Woods
Tormented
The Netherwell Horror

Haunted Series

Inside Perron Manor (Book 0)
Haunted: Perron Manor (Book 1)
Haunted: Devil's Door (Book 2)
Haunted: Purgatory (Book 3)
Haunted: Possession (Book 4)
Haunted: Mother Death (Book 5)
Haunted: Asylum (Book 6)
Haunted: Hotel (Book 7)
Haunted: Catacombs (Book 8)
Haunted: End of Days (Book 9)

Darkfall Series

Darkfall: Deathborn (Book 1)
Darkfall: Shadows of the Deep (Book 2)
Darkfall: Crimson Dawn (Book 3)

Darkfall: Orchard of Flesh (Book 4)

Short Story Collection

Wanna be Scared?

Standalone Books

House of Thorns

ABOUT THE AUTHOR

Lee Mountford is a horror author from the North-East of England. His first book, Horror in the Woods, was published in May 2017 to fantastic reviews, and his follow-up book, The Demonic, achieved Best Seller status in both Occult Horror and British Horror categories on Amazon.

He is a lifelong horror fan, much to the dismay of his amazing wife, Michelle, and his work is available in ebook, print and audiobook formats.

In August 2017 he and his wife welcomed their first daughter, Ella, into the world. In May 2019, their second daughter, Sophie, came along. Michelle is hoping the girls don't inherit their father's love of the macabre, but Lee has other ideas…

For more information
www.leemountford.com
leemountford01@googlemail.com

ACKNOWLEDGMENTS

Thanks first to my amazing Beta Reader Team, who have greatly helped me polish and hone this book:

James Bacon
John Brooks
Nicole Burns
Mary Cavazos-Manos
Karen Day
Jim Donohue
Sally Feliz
Doreene Fernandes
Domenic Fiore
Jenn Freitag
Ursula Gillam
Vicky Gorman
Larry Green
Clayton Hall
Emily Haynes
Dorie Heriot
Lucy Hughes
Monica Julian
Marie K
Dawn Keate
Jon R Kraushar
Paul Letendre
Katrina Lindsay
Diane McCarty
Leanne Pert

Cassandra Pipps
Janalyn Prude
Carley Jessica Pyne
Gale Raab
Laura Rafferty-Aspis
Justin Read
Emelie Rombe
Nicola Jayne Smith
Crystal Mirja Tyrell
Rob Walker
Sharon Watret

Also, a huge thanks to these fantastic people:

My editor, Josiah Davis (www.jdbookservices.com) for such an amazing job as always.

The cover was supplied by Debbie at The Cover Collection.

(www.thecovercollection.com).

I cannot recommend their work enough.

And the last thank you, as always, is the most important. To my amazing family: my wife, Michelle, and my daughters, Ella and Sophie—thank you for everything. You three are my world.

❀ Formatted with Vellum